A TURN
FOR THE
CURSE

PERSEPHONE PRINGLE COZY MYSTERIES: SEVEN

PATTI LARSEN

ISBN: 978-1-998948-34-5

CHAPTER ONE

I turned down the tree-lined drive from the main road, my daughter's continuing stare out the passenger's window only elevating my anxiety. "I'm sure she's fine, Callie," I said, reaching over to first stroke her dark brown curls before giving my fluffy white therapy cat, Belladonna, a scratch behind one ear. Normally, the floof of feline friendliness would have been relegated to her carrier and strapped securely into the back seat. But I'd relented despite how dangerous it was to have her loose in the front, and not because she tended toward the wailing hopelessness of most cats when confined to a small space not of her choosing.

I was far more worried about Calliope's state of mind than Belladonna's.

"I can't believe they wouldn't let us visit for a whole week." Callie's bitterness hadn't relented and had only grown over the last seven days, since her girlfriend and lifelong companion, Thalia Vesterville, had been removed from the hospital and transferred to the specialist treatment facility where she'd been sent to recover from brain surgery. It was still surreal she'd been diagnosed with a brain tumor only two weeks prior, that her surgery had been performed within days of discovery, and that she'd been on the mend since then. Not that you'd know it by the way Calliope pined for her. Considering the pair hadn't been apart more than a few hours over the last two years, the separation had to be agony for my daughter. But more so, I knew, for Thalia, who'd only accepted the transfer on her oncologist's insistence.

"She needed to heal," I said, knowing I didn't sound convincing (because I disagreed completely with their methods) and struggled myself to keep from arguing with Dr. Sandra Jessup who'd recommended the center for Thalia's recouperation. There had been concern about the Vesterville heiress's mental health, and while she could easily have afforded in-home care at the family's palatial estate, Thalia's refusal to return to Vesterville House had sealed the deal. Her lingering belief in the so-called curse that plagued her line was simply a fallacy, but Thalia believed it and that impacted her far greater than was good for her.

Never mind her wayward uncle, Gaines Vesterville, still hadn't made an appearance. While I knew more about him and the truth of who he was than was healthy for me, I'd expected him to show in the dark of night after he'd messaged me back.

I'm on my way.

Apparently, on his way meant in his own good time. I had sent him updates, naturally, and received a few cryptic replies with gratitude for keeping him up to date. But other than that, he'd remained conspicuously absent. I wasn't sure if that was a good thing or a bad thing, or if reaching out to him had been the smart choice. Then again, not telling him wouldn't have gone over well, and despite the circumstances of our last meeting, a small and vain part of me was excited to see the handsome Vesterville again.

Persephone Pringle. Clean your mind, woman.

"This is ridiculous, Mom." Callie huffed a breath into Belladonna's soft, white fur, the cat's green eyes blinking slowly back at her as she chirped her agreement with my daughter. Calliope's hazel eyes met mine, her round face leaned out over the last week, looking far more like her father than ever. The fact Very Special Agent in Charge Trent Garret had barely stopped by once to look in on his daughter or asked after the young woman we'd both cared about since she and Callie became friends wasn't doing him any favors when it came down to it. Maybe it was because our daughter chose to move home instead of remaining alone at Vesterville House while Thalia was indisposed. More likely, however, he had simply moved on.

I didn't know if I'd ever forgive him for that.

Callie had stopped asking and though she was twenty-two now and a full-grown woman who could make her own decisions, she'd been daddy's girl her entire life. His shift of attention from his flesh and blood to his new relationship with Melanie Anderson and her daughter, Brin, had to be taking a toll on my kid as much as this forced separation from the young woman she loved.

"I agree," I said then, the tall, rectangular building just coming into view past the trees giving me a rather institutionalized feeling, like a movie version of some mental hospital haunted by trauma and death. I felt goosebumps rise at the sight but shoved my trepidation aside. This was a treatment center, nothing more, likely repurposed from some old facility. I parked in the small side lot, the autumn sun bright in the blue sky, belying the chill in the November air. "But we're here now and Thalia's going to be all right." I squeezed her hand this time after turning off the engine, fixing my kid with a steady and confident stare despite the fact I had no idea what we were walking into. Not seeing Thalia was only part of their treatment recommendation. Callie hadn't even been allowed to call her or message via text.

"She'd better be," Callie snarled. Then caught her breath, reaching behind her for the carrier. Belladonna's ears flattened a moment, but she entered the confined space after little hesitation. Maybe she'd learned fighting it wasn't going to get her anywhere? More likely, she sensed our unrest and decided not to add to it. Bella settled on the padded

4

bottom of her temporary prison while Callie zipped it shut. "I really appreciate this, Mom."

"I love Lia too," I said, fighting the sting of tears in my eyes, the thickness in my throat. I'd known Thalia forever, had practically raised her alongside Callie when her parents died tragically. "I'm sorry I couldn't do more."

"What did Dr. Renfrew say?" Callie climbed out of the car with Belladonna's carrier in her hands and I joined her, locking the SUV behind us with a soft beeping as the alarm activated, sliding my arm around my daughter's shoulders, feeling her tension even through the puffy blue coat she wore. A stiff breeze shoved us from behind, whipping some leaves into a tiny whirlwind, chasing us up the wide, stone steps to the glass doors of the center.

"I have temporary privileges," I said, grateful that my old colleague and classmate, Dr. Richard Renfrew, had managed to wrangle my credentials at the facility. He owed me, after all, for assisting one of his patients and solving her murder. "Now that we're here, I'll take over Thalia's care. It's going to be all right."

Callie's skepticism didn't disappear altogether, but her cheeks weren't quite so pale and there was hope in her eyes. Now, as long as Thalia was well...

Not going there. Not until I saw her with my own eyes.

CHAPTER TWO

"May I help you?" The orderly who approached from behind the front desk towered over both of us, the silver nametag on his light blue scrubs identifying him as Jose.

"Persephone Pringle," I said in no uncertain tone and terms, chin up, professionalism vibrating from every pore because I read attitude in his face, and he could take that and shove it. "Thalia Vesterville's personal therapist. We're expected."

His hesitation told me he didn't get the memo, but that wasn't going to stop me, believe it. Now that we were here? Nothing would keep me from Thalia.

"Dr. Pringle." A tall, dark-haired older man in glasses and a white lab coat hurried from a narrow corridor, one hand outstretched. The orderly backed off, head down, though his full lips thinned out and a distinctly dissatisfied expression gave him a sullen look I wasn't fond of. "Dr. Amir Yonan. Richard speaks so highly of you."

"Dr. Yonan." I shook the man's hand, gesturing to my daughter. "This is Calliope, Thalia's partner, and my therapy cat, Belladonna." Bella let out a soft cry from inside the carrier. "We're eager to see Thalia, doctor. I need to assess her current state immediately."

"Of course." Dr. Yonan's stiff nod and weak smile weren't encouraging. "This way, please." He led me past the orderly whose dark glare followed his boss a moment before the hulking man turned and strode off. Yonan, meanwhile, carried on speaking as we hurried to keep up. "Welcome to The Recovery Center," he said. "I hope your drive was pleasant."

"You're only an hour from Wallace," I said. "It went by fast enough. I'm deeply concerned with Thalia's isolation, Dr. Yonan. As her primary therapist, I should have been granted contact with my patient. This is most irregular and distressing. I hope Thalia's stay here wasn't a mistake."

Dr. Yonan's briefest pause had me anxious all over again. "Ms. Vesterville's physical recovery has been excellent, Dr. Pringle," he said. "She's had the best care here."

"And her mental state?" I wasn't letting him off the hook. I'd allowed this because Dr. Jessup recommended the place, but you could bet I'd be taking steps if Thalia was in any way under duress.

"I assure you," he said, "we're doing everything

we can for her. Our methods might be unusual, but they have been proven to aid in recovery far more quickly than standard care." We'd left the large, cold lobby of stone and entered a hallway, white with large paintings on the walls, less a hospital feel in the corridor than some expensive hotel, with doorways flanking the walls marked with numbers and housing chart holders beneath. "Ms. Vesterville's mental health has been troublesome, I admit. But with her physical recovery now assured, I'm sure you and Ms. Garret will find her full recovery swift and to your satisfaction."

I was liking this less and less. "Considering the fact Thalia's mental state had much improved after her surgery due to the relief of pressure on her brain, I'd have expected her to be well on the way to healed in that regard as well, Dr. Yonan." He paused by a doorway, turning to me while I scowled at him, arms crossed over my chest. "The only reason I agreed to allow Thalia to be placed in this facility was because of that recovery. Are you telling me now that I was in error and your forced week of seclusion has degraded her health?"

He licked his lips, visibly agitated, though he did his best to hide it. "Our staff therapists have been unable to ascertain any issues," he said. "Thus, I can only assume some swelling remains after her surgery that's complicating matters."

Callie muttered something under her breath, but I prodded her with one elbow because it was probably full of swearwords and there was only one way to get through to someone like Dr. Amir Yonan.

Except, we were interrupted before I could offer my own thoughts on the matter. The sound of a harsh laugh had me turning, frowning at the young man who lounged back in the wheelchair in which he sat, expensive robe wrapped around him far too much velvet for someone in their early twenties. The young woman who pushed him wore one of her own, clearly not a member of staff.

"Mr. Wyatt." Dr. Yonan stepped away from me, gesturing to the pair. "Ms. Teres, you're not to be acting as an orderly for Mr. Wyatt."

"Nora doesn't mind, doc," the arrogant Wyatt said, tilting his head to give first Callie, then me, the up and down with a cynical smirk on his face. "Newcomers? How fun."

"I'll summon Jose at once," Dr. Yonan said, though Wyatt waved him off.

"Don't bother," he said. "Mush, Nora. Good dog." He laughed again, the young woman flushing dark red, her black hair in a messy ponytail at the nape of her neck doing nothing to hide her furious expression.

Dr. Yonan spluttered but finally composed himself, still faintly vibrating with frustration.

"My trust in your facility hasn't increased," I said.

His dark eyes flashed with something not quite angry but on the border of resentment that had me determined to remove Thalia from this place ASAP.

"Ms. Vesterville's room is here," he said, no longer trying to be polite.

"Finally," I said, answering with my own cheek. "And if I find this choice of treatment has instead harmed Ms. Vesterville," I said, voice cold and jaw tight, "I assure you this recovery center of yours will be hearing from her lawyers. Now, if you'll excuse us." Callie was already pushing past both of us, the door whipping open in her free hand, my daughter hurrying inside.

I followed more slowly, though I wanted to rush, too, unwilling, however, to show even a scrap of weakness to Dr. Yonan. When I finally did enter, Calliope was already at the bed, arms around the sobbing young woman tucked under the covers, Belladonna meowing for freedom.

But it was Thalia's almost incoherent state that had me stopping in my tracks, the Vesterville heiress writhing in Callie's arms.

"Go away!" She pushed my daughter off her, face contorting as she shrieked loudly enough to make Belladonna fall silent. "What are you doing here? I don't know you. I don't want you. Get out!"

Thalia wasn't better. She was worse than before her tumor.

Someone was getting sued.

CHAPTER THREE

Dr. Yonan's first reaction? He spun and left the room. And while I judged him instantly for running off like that, part of me was grateful he'd vanished because it was not only clear to me Thalia was in terrible hands here and we'd made a horrific choice agreeing to this arrangement, but she was better off with me than that fraud who'd fled the scene of this crime.

To say I was angry? The understatement of the century. Something I forced myself to put aside as I hurried toward Calliope and Thalia, the cat carrier on the foot of the bed now erupting with the frenzy Belladonna rarely deployed unless she was in panic mode herself. And while letting her out might not have been the best choice, I relied on my instincts and training and unzipped the front of the bag, freeing my cat before joining my daughter at her girlfriend's side.

Belladonna immediately exited the carrier with her tail high and a plaintive string of mews trailing along with her as she strode with her characteristic confidence up Thalia's legs and firmly planted herself in the young woman's lap. Fearless and commanding, she pawed at Thalia until the stricken Vesterville finally looked down and met those intense green eyes.

They'd always shared a bond, I knew that. It was the main reason Belladonna came with me in the first place. But I had no idea until that moment just how strong Thalia's attachment was. With a low cry, she gathered the fluffy white cat into her arms and sobbed into Belladonna's fur, her struggles over but weeping just as troubling as her incoherency had been.

Calliope looked up over Thalia's bent head to meet my gaze, her face sheathed in tears, cheeks bright pink and unable to speak though her throat worked, and her lips moved as though she made the effort. I reached across the trembling young woman beside me to take my daughter's hand while gently stroking Thalia's hair.

"Everything is going to be all right," I said in my most confident therapist voice, though my heart wrenched at the sight of my two kids in such a state. Belladonna purred loudly, letting out a soft cheep of agreement, before nuzzling Thalia's face with her own. Her support bolstered me like nothing else could have. "We're taking you home, Thalia," I said.

Callie gulped and nodded, wiping at her face with both hands and smearing them on the bed sheets in a rapid movement. "It's going to be okay, Lia," she managed to say at last, voice thick and lower lip trembling but with her own determination rising at last. "We love you and we're going to take care of you."

Thalia looked up slowly, eyes bloodshot and almost empty, though when she locked her gaze on me, she blinked before turning her head and seeing Calliope there as though for the first time.

"Callie?" Thalia sobbed my daughter's name before hugging her with one arm, Belladonna still tucked against her with the other. "What... when did you get here?"

I shook my head at Calliope when her eyes flickered to me, and she took the silent warning to heart.

"Just now, love," she said, voice soft, fingers brushing over Thalia's cheek. "We came to take you home."

"Yes, please," Thalia whispered, leaning into her. "I'm so tired, Callie. So tired."

And I was so freaking done already.

Footsteps hurried toward the door, spinning me around, just as Dr. Yonan and the burly orderly, Jose, rushed inside. I spotted the syringe in hand and immediately put myself between the two men and Thalia, knowing very well I had the kind of scowl that could label me as trouble and not caring even a little bit because they didn't know trouble yet.

Oh, but they would. They *would*.

Insert Momma Bear growling here.

Dr. Yonan spoke before I could. "Ms. Vesterville needs sedation for her own protection." Even as he said it, he seemed to notice she'd calmed and that she no longer sounded out of touch with herself. That hesitation was all the maneuvering room I needed to shut him down.

"As you can see," I said with no little level of sarcasm layered on for good measure, "with *proper* care," you better believe I said that, "and the *right* kind of therapy," I said what I said, come at me bro, "Ms. Vesterville is not only stable, she's markedly improved from what you've been able to accomplish." I paused. "*Dr.* Yonan." Because his title was clearly questionable.

Mic. Freaking. Drop.

The doctor's expression settled into sullen resentment. "This is my facility, Dr. Pringle," he said. "You are a guest here with privileges I granted you." Really? He wanted to go that way, did he? "And Ms. Vesterville has been placed under my care."

This was going to be fun. The truth was clearly a giant surprise for him, poor baby.

"By *me*," I said. He blinked while I crossed my arms over my chest. The fact he had no idea I had power of attorney in Thalia's affairs while she recovered made me doubt him even further. "That's about to be revoked." I let him nibble on that a second before delivering the final blow. "And your facility investigated for your choice of practice." I gestured at the syringe in Jose's hand, the bulky orderly hovering behind his boss, looking back and forth between us but without a hint of humanity on his face. "If your idea of psychiatric recovery is about drugs and sedation, Dr. Yonan, you and I have very different beliefs when it comes to treating patients."

Yonan spluttered, but he had to know he was on thin ice and didn't have a leg to support him if I kicked it out from under him. Which I planned to do, pronto.

"I'm also Thalia's primary therapist," I said, "and I've been kept out of her healing process far too long, something that is terribly apparent to me now. I'll be delivering a full report to Dr. Sandra Jessup as well as my colleague, Dr. Renfrew, about the state of your treatments. And if I catch you dosing Thalia one more time, I'll have the family's lawyers here and you shut down so fast you'll be scraping your behind off the sidewalk." I turned away from him. "Now get out and prepare Thalia's discharge papers. Immediately."

It took him a moment to comply, but he finally did, both sets of footsteps retreating. I rejoined the girls and Belladonna, the cat's steady purr softening as Thalia sagged backward into her pillows, pale face near translucence, so thin I could see the ridges of her breastbone through her white skin, count every vein in her hands. She'd never been a sturdy woman by any means but seeing her so drawn and weak troubled me very much.

"I can't go home," she whispered, voice cracking, tears running from the corners of her eyes.

"You're not staying here," Calliope said with a

firm nod to me.

"We'll figure it out," I told Thalia, stroking her thin hair out of her bangs. Dr. Jessup had shaved a large square in the back, but had done her best, she told me, to keep the bare patch underneath so Thalia could cover it. The rough ponytail she wore showed the edges of it, and while the incision from the surgery appeared to be healing well, I couldn't help but wonder if something had gone awry after Dr. Jessup closed her up.

One way to find out. "Thalia, when was your last MRI?"

She stared at me, a bit dazed. "The hospital," she said.

Was she freaking kidding me? "Have you had any tests since you arrived?" It was so hard not to blow up, to clench my jaw and speak in a reasonable tone.

"I don't know," she whispered. "I don't remember much."

Which meant they'd been keeping her sedated. How was that beneficial or healthy? My estimation of Dr. Jessup plummeted if she had any idea what kind of horror show Amir Yonan was running here. I couldn't believe she knew the extent, but she'd be finding out, believe you me.

The whole world would if I had any say about it.

CHAPTER FOUR

Once I was confident Thalia wasn't going to melt down again, Calliope seated next to her on the bed with her arms around her, Belladonna happily snuggled in her lap, I left the three of them to go in search of Dr. Yonan and Thalia's discharge paperwork. It was difficult not to berate myself for allowing the young woman I adored to fall into this kind of situation. I knew better than to place blame when I'd acted out of the belief that I was doing what would help her heal the fastest. And yet, as I strode back toward the main lobby, my heart pounding and my temper barely in check, I fought my own tears at the truth of the matter.

I'd let Thalia down. I hadn't vetted this place personally and allowed the Vesterville heiress to wallow here for far longer than she should have. Any anger I felt was aimed at myself, I assure you, though it was going to come out at others, I had no doubt if I didn't take a moment and use some of my own healing tools to calm my temper and get myself under control.

Which was what I finally did to prevent bursting out into the open and unfolding a tantrum of epic proportions. Just before I cleared the hallway into the lobby, I pushed my way through a door marked MAINTENANCE and shoved it shut behind me, leaning with my back against it and catching my breath through sobs that wanted to escape.

How could Dr. Jessup even suggest this was a good idea? Why did I let Thalia fall into Yonan's hands like this? What was wrong with that man? I'd have his license for this. And what was wrong with me, abandoning the young woman who'd been as much a daughter to me as Callie to suffer without fighting for her like I should have—like no one in her own family ever had?

It took longer than a few minutes, about twenty passing by the time I dabbed at the tears on my face and managed a long, slow exhale. All the pressure in my chest released as I ran through a cycle of emotional tools, knowing there would be red spots on my face and collarbone where I used tapping to urge the emotional onslaught to rise and express. It was worth it, however. As I righted myself and squared my shoulders, still trembling a little but no longer overcome with anger and shame, I knew I was in a better headspace not only to confront Yonan for his part in this debacle but to do so from a healthy and powerful place instead of one driven by hysterics.

If there was one thing I learned as a woman of a certain age, men didn't respond well to overly emotional confrontations, and nothing would put me at a disadvantage with the doctor in charge than losing my temper or crying in front of him. Thalia deserved my best and that was what she was going to get from now on.

I emerged from the glorified closet with a firm shove to the door, chin up, ready to get what Thalia needed, only to squeak in surprise when I almost ran right into the orderly. Jose stopped in his tracks when I nodded to him, because a visiting therapist walking out of a maintenance room was surely nothing out of the ordinary, right? Instead of allowing him time to contemplate—which he was doing from the way his eyes narrowed and lips thinned—I jumped on a question.

"I need to see Thalia's chart," I said. "And I wanted to talk about her drug regimen."

"You'll have to ask Dr. Yonan about that," Jose said after a long and uncomfortable pause. He shuffled his feet, white sneakers squeaking on the tile floor where the heavy beige carpeting hadn't yet begun.

"I'm asking you," I said. "What's your last name, please?"

Another bout of hesitation followed though he did finally respond. "Delgato," he said, rather sullen response not earning him any points with me.

"Mr. Delgato," I said, "Thalia is my patient and as I have power of attorney in her case, you can't refuse my request." I waited for him to process that, caught his brief nod and faintly frustrated huff of a sigh before I pressed on. "Has Ms. Vesterville been sedated often since her arrival?"

He looked down, stuffing both hands into the pockets of his scrubs. "She seemed fine when she was first admitted," he said. "But that night she suffered a psychotic episode and we had to sedate her. Since then, Dr. Yonan has her on a course of anti-psychotics and anti-depressants. When she gets agitated, we sedate her." He shrugged like what he told me was no big deal even though it was a huge deal, thank you.

All that time in the closet treating my temper? Was well on the way to being useless. I managed to catch myself before I freaked out, however, and exhaled long and slow between the urge to smack him and needing to carry on asking questions. Questions won.

"Has she had a recent MRI?" In her condition and treated with such heavy medication, it was possible she had but didn't recall.

Jose shook his head. "Not as far as I know," he said. "Check with Dr. Yonan."

Ridiculous. "So, a patient who's had recent brain surgery that altered her mental state is degrading in your care and no one thought to have another scan done?" I tsked, wanting to do more than that while the truly unhelpful man in front of me stared at the floor with his sullen scowl infuriating me further. It

20

was clear to me I wasn't going to get much more out of him either, Jose's gaze flickering down the hallway and body swaying like he intended to dash the second I let him go.

He wasn't my target of choice anyway. I waved him off and hurried to carry on to the office and my discussion with his boss, knowing I really needed to step off again but pretty positive if I did it would take an epic session of therapies to bring me down from the anger I now felt roiling around inside me.

Dr. Yonan would just have to deal with raging Persephone Pringle and heaven help us both if he gave me an ounce of lip.

The security guard at the desk wasn't happy about my stomping approach, the young man in uniform leaping up from his seat and confronting me before I could pass him and enter the hall behind him where OFFICES was marked clearly over the entry.

"I'm sorry, you can't go back there," he said. At least he seemed earnest and nice enough, if firm in his denial, one hand rising to hold me back without touching me. I met his black eyes, noted the faint sheen of sweat rising on his dark skin, and took a little pity on him.

"Persephone Pringle," I said, not quite snapping, but close enough, "personal therapist of Thalia Vesterville. I'm taking my patient out of this facility." He inhaled with alarm on his face, glancing over his shoulder at the hallway to the offices, but I wasn't done. "Tell Dr. Yonan he and I will have our conversation as soon as I have Thalia placed in more appropriate care." I spun on my heel then and headed back to Thalia and Calliope. I even had myself convinced by the time I hit the carpeting of her hallway that this was the best possible outcome. I didn't have to spew my emotional overflow onto the man and Thalia would be safe in my care. I'd have time to arrange myself sufficiently to deal with Dr. Yonan and this facility without throwing the kind of hissy fit that would damage my professional reputation all while satisfying my need to ensure the likes of Amir Yonan never harmed another patient again.

CHAPTER FIVE

I was already to Thalia's door and entering with my plan in motion in my head and Yonan's downfall assured when I realized two things. One, Callie wasn't in the room any longer and despite that fact, Thalia wasn't alone.

Belladonna perched in her lap, tail thrashing, hissing softly under her breath, green eyes narrowed and focused on the young man in the wheelchair who sat at Thalia's bedside, the same young man I'd seen earlier. The young woman who'd been pushing his chair stood off to one side, head down and cheeks deeply red, clearly distressed. The sight of them, Thalia's pale cheeks sunken, fresh tears on her face augmenting her upset, froze me in mid-step and gave me a hint of just what kind of treatment she was actually receiving in this revolting place.

"Too bad that tumor didn't blow," he was laughing. "Then you'd be all the way brain dead instead of just a waste of time. At least vegetables are useful." He snickered as Thalia sobbed once. "You're nothing, Vesterville," he hissed at her then, leaning forward with his profile twisting into hateful rancor as pronounced as his tone of voice. "Maybe someone will do you a favor and put you out of your pathetic misery."

Oh. My. God.

I thought I was angry before. I had no idea just how furious I could get. Except I surprised myself. Because rather than a raging torrent of free-flowing magma emerging from me to consume the young man and everything he held dear, icy cold wrapped me in a shroud of concentrated power that might have looked contained and controlled from the outside but felt so far out of my wheelhouse I almost took a step back.

Didn't, though. Because *Thalia.*

"I don't know who you are," I said, not recognizing my own voice, though the tone of it clearly caught the attention of both visitors and Thalia, the three looking up in shock, Belladonna's hissing turning to a low growl of warning, "and I don't really care. If you don't leave this room immediately, I'll ensure you never leave it." I stepped aside and gestured at the exit. "You have five seconds."

I caught the petulance in his face, the flash of nervousness he smothered in resentful rebellion.

Even noted despite the chill around me he might have been handsome if he wasn't so very evil, cruelty and malice emanating from him like a beacon. And while as a therapist I knew such a person was either a product of his environment and had suffered horrifically to become who he was, or instead was a victim himself of physiology and biological and chemical issues that altered his brain and ended any chance for him to develop normally, I couldn't manage to muster any kind of professional distance or understanding. That was on me, and didn't say much for me when it came to my ethical responsibility as a therapist, but honestly?

I was so done I could taste it.

Before the young man could protest, his blue eyes narrowing, pretty face scrunching while he inhaled to respond, the young woman with him lurched forward and grasped the handles of his chair, spinning him and pushing hard, carrying both of them out of the room and into the hallway beyond. The sound of him yelling at her lasted for quite some time, though the words were muffled aside from the recognizable use of Thalia's name, and I quite frankly didn't give a cat's tail about what he thought of his forced exit.

Thalia wept silently, stroking Belladonna's fur. My cat's grumbling had gone silent, though her purr had as yet to return. I joined Thalia on the bed, my own hands shaking as the cold subsided, rush of my renewed emotions making my breath hitch.

"The curse," Thalia muttered, words slurring enough I had to strain to make her out. "It's

following me everywhere, Seph. I'll never escape it."
She shuddered, head tilting to one side and when I
met her eyes and caught the glaze in them, my rage
was renewed.

Despite my orders, Dr. Yonan had dosed her.
She was clearly high. And I'd had enough of this to
last me a lifetime.

"Mom." Callie's voice behind me held shock. I
turned to find her hurrying toward us, a glass of
water in one hand. "What happened?" It was
obvious she'd overheard some of what the young
man was yelling. She stopped in her tracks at the
sight of Thalia's lean and how she'd started
muttering, a thin line of drool forming in the corner
of her mouth. I quickly wiped it clean with a tissue,
Calliope's hazel eyes huge and filling with tears.

"We'll have to wait for this dose to wear off," I
said through gritted teeth. There was no way I would
risk transporting Thalia in my car. Or we could get
an ambulance. She could certainly afford it. "Never
mind," I said, waving off Callie's inhale to protest.
"I've got it covered."

"Mom, where are we going to take her?" My
daughter's distress only increased as Thalia began
humming to herself, fingers now barely moving as
she tried to pat Belladonna. My cat surprised me,
slinking away from Thalia's touch and toward the
carrier still at the foot of the bed, hiding inside and
laying down to watch us from the relative safety of
the interior.

"I'm going to call Dr. Jessup and tell her what's
going on," I said. "We'll try to get her readmitted to

the hospital in Wallace." I hugged Callie, my own emotions set aside for my daughter's welfare. "I know taking her to the estate isn't the best option, but we can hire her the best care."

She shook her head, pulling away. "Can't we take her home to your house?" My daughter had grown up in so many ways and had a solid stubborn streak I admired very much, but she also had her father's worry-wart nature. It had been a long time since I'd heard her sound so young and vulnerable, even through all of this mess with Thalia. That plea in her eyes, in her words, in the way she clutched my hands, had me nodding and agreeing even if it was a terrible idea. "I can take care of her. And we can have nurses and all the things." She hugged me hard when I nodded again. "Mom, she needs us, not a hospital. And Vesterville House..."

I sighed deeply, releasing all of my anger and sorrow and blame. "Being at Vesterville House will only make her healing harder," I said. "Okay, Callie. We'll try it. Let's take Thalia home." At least, for the moment. Because I now feared we'd be back at the hospital in short order. Something was terribly wrong with Thalia that hiding at my house wouldn't fix. But giving my daughter a win at the moment? Priceless.

The last thing I expected was a knock on the door. I turned, triggered and ready for a battle, only to spot two young people peeking inside, both of them appearing as concerned as I felt.

"I'm so sorry to interrupt," the young man said, his dark hair falling over his deep brown eyes, raising one hand as I waved for him to enter. The girl at his side hovered at his elbow, biting her lower lip as she held onto his arm for support. She seemed as thin and wasted as Thalia, stringy blonde hair in a tight ponytail over one shoulder, huge eyes pale, dark circles under them and sunken cheeks giving her an ethereal appearance. "We're worried about Thalia and wanted to check on her." He gestured at the young woman beside him. "This is Faith and I'm Luca. We're friends." His expression hardened as he looked back over his shoulder a moment. "I take it Asher was here."

I nodded, waited for more. Which Luca delivered a moment later. After taking a step forward, Faith joining him in a rush, the young man's expression flickering out of concern and into anger.

"Thalia's not getting better," he blurted like he didn't expect to be believed, "but it's not her fault. I can't prove it or anything," Faith shook her head to agree with him, "but Asher's been messing with her head and if she's worse? It's his fault."

CHAPTER SIX

Considering what I'd just witnessed, I wasn't inclined to disagree, though from what I'd seen of Thalia's state, being bullied was far from all of what she faced.

"I'm Callie," my daughter said, leaving her girlfriend's side long enough to shake both of their hands. They seemed surprised by the offer, though Calliope's old-fashioned ways were a reflection of her upbringing by a pair of professionals who valued good manners.

"Thalia talks about you all the time." Faith's breathy voice had me worrying about her, even if she seemed steady enough with Luca to help her. He guided her toward a chair and eased her down into it, the young woman exhaling softly and squeezing his hand in thanks. "It's so nice to finally meet you."

"Thanks for looking in on her," Callie said. "Has he been mean to her the whole time she's been here?"

Luca's face contorted, aging him past his early twenties into someone darker and with more serious experiences than his rather round, babyish and sweet face suggested. "Asher likes to pick a target and do his best to make trouble." The way he said it had me wondering if Luca himself had been the focus of bullying, possibly by Asher. "She's so nice, you know. He hates that."

"We do know," I said. "Has anyone reported the activity to Dr. Yonan?" One more strike against the man, honestly.

"We try," Faith said, Luca shrugging, "but nothing seems to come of it." She appeared troubled by that. "We've tried to make sure Thalia's not alone with him."

"It's hard," Luca said, fists clenched at his sides. What demon was he wrestling inside himself that he held his body so rigid and controlled? "Asher makes sure no one witnesses anything, and he has influence here."

Did he now? "We appreciate you trying," I said.

"Are you here to take Thalia away?" Faith's face crumpled, a tear escaping before she wiped it clear. "If you are, don't forget her plants."

Plants? I was well aware of Thalia's passion for all things flora, including the very dangerous garden of poisonous growths housed on the Vesterville estate grounds, but plants here?

"She rescued some from the lobby and a few of the staff gave her theirs from their offices," Faith said, still breathy but with more enthusiasm. "There's a little greenhouse in the back and she's been keeping them there."

Just like Thalia. "I'll see what I can do," I said.

The two exchanged looks before Luca sighed. "She's so happy when she's in the greenhouse," he said. "That's why Asher targets her so much. He thinks it makes her weak."

I bet it did. But the thought gave me an idea. "Can you show us where the greenhouse is?" I motioned to Callie, then Thalia. "Maybe we could take her there, sweetie, and give her some fresh air and a moment to come back to herself while I figure out what to do next."

Calliope immediately went to the corner under the window and retrieved the folded wheelchair there, Luca expertly popping it open for her when she struggled with the process.

"Thanks," she said, while Thalia clapped her hands in a thin show of excitement, glazed eyes flickering around the room, smile of a lost child making my heart ache.

"Are we going out?" She struggled with the sheets, Calliope catching her and helping her into the wheelchair, Thalia's blue silk pajamas bunching around her legs. I adjusted her clothing, turning to close up Belladonna's carrier and hefting it again. I could have left her behind, but there was no way that was happening. I refused to give Asher or anyone else the opportunity to tamper with my cat, thank you.

"Lead on," I said. "I'd really love to see this greenhouse."

It wasn't far to walk, further down the corridor and around a corner, through a doorway into the back of the building. The two guides moved slowly, Faith finally agreeing to a wheelchair of her own that Luca retrieved from what had to be her room. We made better time then, reaching the exit in question. I noted it was near the stairwell, steps leading up and down. It was darker here, feeling more industrial than the polished and expensive tastes that dominated the residential hallways.

Luca noted my attention and nodded in the direction of the steps. "There are more rooms upstairs," he said, "but first floor is reserved for those of us who can afford it." He wrinkled his nose like that offended him, but it made his words crystal clear. Wealthy patients got the best care, good to know. Or were kept sick to ensure continuing contributions to the center's coffers? I was now starting to wonder. And yes, that was my mind running off on tangents, but I'd heard of stranger things happening. With Thalia clearly not having direct family to care for her, had Yonan seen an opportunity to maximize his payment? I wasn't putting anything past him at this point. "Downstairs is the recreation space, a gym, the pool, that kind of stuff. Right here." He reached for the door handle, the glowing EXIT sign over it eerily red in the dimmer hallway.

I followed him through, noting that the concrete

steps down to the little greenhouse had been covered in glass, the humidity inside warmer than the November day, thin sunlight doing a good job behind the green-tinted walls to keep the plants within happy and growing.

Thalia slowly pushed herself out of her chair, accepting my help down the steps lined with pots of what looked like ordinary grasses transplanted for Thalia's benefit, though she ignored them and instead beamed at the more exotic plants on the long tables below. It frustrated me there was no ramp to speak of and I worried she'd been forced to walk these stairs alone, especially if this condition I found her in now was common for her. But she seemed able enough, if dreamily absent, her humming returning when we reached the dirt bottom. She pulled away and went immediately to one of the potted plants, fingers stroking the leaves of what looked like an aloe. Since I wasn't much of a green thumb myself, I didn't strive to identify any of the rescues Thalia managed, only grateful she'd had some outlet to keep her happy during her stay.

The others joined us, and I stepped back, Calliope talking quietly with Luca and Faith while I pulled out my phone and made two calls in quick succession. The first, to Dr. Jessup, ended in a voicemail. I left a very firm message before dialing Richard, only to get the same result. I did my best not to go off on Yonan to my colleague, knowing he didn't always respect my way of doing things, but needing to share with someone else in the field who could perhaps do a little digging for me behind the scenes while I was too busy with Thalia to do it myself. The fact Richard hadn't red-flagged The Recovery Center when he'd helped me arrange my privileges told me either nothing popped up or he hadn't checked. Since either was possible (both were, to be honest), I didn't hold it against him as much as I was Dr. Jessup.

As much. Because I was willy nilly at the moment when it came to blame.

I briefly considered emailing Gaines again and decided against it. Until I knew for certain what was going on with Thalia, there was no way I could justify telling a spy and assassin his niece was in deeper trouble thanks to me and my neglect (I know, I know). The last thing I wanted was a string of dead bodies (Dr. Yonan and Dr. Jessup among them) before my own joined theirs if Gaines decided Thalia's condition warranted revenge. I'd already seen firsthand how he dealt with those he deemed traitors to him and those he loved. Sure, I wasn't happy either, but at least I wasn't homicidal.

Yet.

That situation? About to be challenged. Because as I hovered over my email app, debating Gaines and even Trent (would the FBI be helpful in this case?), the door at the top of the stairs opened and the sound of nasty laughter had my blood boiling all over again.

"Oh, look," Asher said in a simpering whine meant to mimic childishness, "she's playing with her dirt again." His vicious hate couldn't seem to cut through Thalia's present distraction, however, so for once I was glad Dr. Yonan disobeyed me and dosed her.

"You're not welcome here," I said, striding to the bottom of the stairs. I noted the girl was still with him, the dark-haired shadow who always seemed to be behind his wheelchair. He'd called her Nora, right? "Either of you."

She flinched as if unhappy to be noticed or called out. I was surprised when Luca joined me, though he stood a bit back from me, just visible in my periphery.

"Leave her alone, Asher." His voice shook, but when I glanced his way, I saw Luca's determination and anger, hands fisted again, jaw jumping.

"Make me," Asher shot back, arrogance unrepentant. "Oh, right, you tried before and failed because you're a *loser*." He laughed at that, devoid of humor. "Shut up and sit down. No one cares what you think."

Luca wavered next to me but didn't retreat to his credit.

As for me? Asher could try to bully me all he wanted, but the kid was clearly deluded if he thought he was going to get away with pushing me around.

Maybe I would have gone overboard and said something I shouldn't have to someone barely past twenty, but whether I would have regretted that outburst or not wasn't something I was in a position to find out. Because as I opened my mouth to send him packing, Dr. Yonan appeared at the door himself, frowning at the scene.

"Mr. Wyatt," the doctor said to Asher who barely

spared him a glance, "you're due for your hydrotherapy session. I suggest you make your way there now, please."

"Stay out of this," Asher snarled at him like Dr. Yonan was a servant, not a psychiatrist. That surprised me more than anything and cooled my temper with the weight of curiosity because no way did an upstart jerk like Asher Wyatt get away with talking to Dr. Yonan like that. "Hey, plant girl." Thalia twitched just a little, her humming fading. "You love your green stuff, huh?" He let out a barking laugh. "We'll see how much when I'm done with them. Let's go." He tried to wheel himself but caught a hiss of a breath as he favored one arm. The young woman behind his chair immediately lurched forward to catch the handles and turn him herself. Dr. Yonan stepped aside and scowled after the pair, but not before Nora looked up at last and met Luca's eyes.

Whatever passed between them, it was intensely personal and had the young man beside me dropping his gaze and his aggression while the pair disappeared.

"That," I snapped at Dr. Yonan, "was unacceptable and one more reason I'm taking Thalia out of this place immediately."

"You can't," he blurted. "I've just spoken to Dr. Jessup. She wants an MRI done today and until that's complete, Thalia must remain here." He paused then, pained expression on his face. "Please, for her own good."

He had no right to speak those words. But an

MRI might tell me what was going on and since the alternative meant a long ambulance ride to the hospital and possibly a long wait for the test...

"Fine," I snapped, "but I'm staying and so is my daughter and if you do anything to interfere with me, with Thalia, or create any roadblocks to her care and my full cooperation, we're done."

Yonan nodded once before spinning and retreating, the door closing behind him.

Why did I get the feeling I'd just made a terrible decision?

CHAPTER SEVEN

"He really is a good person, you know." I looked behind me to find Faith hovering near, wavering on her feet, her chair left behind upstairs with Thalia's and her gaze locked on the now-closed door. I almost choked on her suggestion but realized it wasn't Asher she was talking about. "Dr. Yonan does his best, but his hands are tied."

"Why do you say that?" I turned to face her, Luca doing the same, while Faith flushed a little.

"I just... he's not..." she didn't seem able to answer my question which had me frowning a little. Luca interrupted my train of thought with his own grim ones.

"I feel bad about Thalia," he said, hands deep in the pockets of his jeans. I had no idea what brought him here to the treatment facility because from what I could tell, Luca was perfectly healthy. Whatever his reason, guilt appeared far more potent than any illness, at least at the moment. "I used to be Asher's target before she got here. I'm sorry she has to put up with his crap." Luca's face fell. "If I was just a little stronger..."

Faith closed the distance between them in two shaking steps, Luca reaching out to catch and support her. "It's not your fault," she said. "You're a good person, Luca. You shouldn't have to stand up to him. Something should be done." Her lips pursed, eyes narrowing.

He shrugged like her words had little impact. "If I was my father's son," he said, "I'd have seen that something done." What did that mean exactly? Luca blew out a long breath before perking a little. "At least it sounds like Thalia's going to get the help she needs."

I nodded at that but wasn't ready to be distracted from the Asher problem just yet. "Why hasn't Dr. Yonan done anything about the bullying?" And why did he let the young man talk to him like that? Asher clearly had no worries about repercussions.

"The Wyatts built this place," Faith said, hands clutching at Luca's bicep to keep her steady.

Ah. Now I understood completely. "Dr. Yonan's job is in their hands," I said.

Neither responded but they didn't have to, did they? And even more reason to get Thalia somewhere safe. Because it was now clear to me no matter what Asher Wyatt did, punishment wasn't going to be forthcoming and having her in a state of constant torment wasn't going to help matters.

Why had I let her come here unsupervised again?

"I'd better get Faith back to her room," Luca said, concerned frown on his face as she wavered again.

"I'm sorry," the young woman whispered. "I'm really tired all of a sudden."

I thanked them both again and watched him guide her up the stairs, disappearing behind the door. Callie sat where she'd been all along, on one of the tables, facing Thalia who continued to putter with the plants there. Calliope had let Belladonna out of her carrier, the cat playing with the leaves of a plant while Thalia laughed, a lovely sound I'd worried I'd never hear from her again. A bit buoyed by the news a brain scan was imminent, I answered my phone when it rang without the tense and angry emotional state I'd been carrying around with me since my arrival.

Which meant when Dr. Sandra Jessup greeted me with concern in her voice, I didn't lose my mind.

"Ms. Pringle, I'm so sorry." She sounded genuine enough. "I've touched base with Dr. Yonan, but I'm not satisfied with the answers I received."

"That makes two of us," I said, sighing softly as tension released. At least she wasn't doubling down and defending the man.

"He came with the highest recommendation, as did his treatment center," she said. "I'm worried because the MRI Thalia had before she left was clear and she was much improved."

"I agree," I said, keeping my voice down though I watched the girls from the other end of the greenhouse for what little privacy that afforded me. The sight of them chatting and Belladonna playing was almost too much for me, because how could they look so happy when things had gone so wrong? "The fact she's been deteriorating, and nothing was done…"

"I've ordered an immediate MRI," she said. "I understand you're going to discharge Thalia and I don't blame you. However, if you could wait until after the scan is sent to me so I can read it…? We have no idea what we're dealing with and if she's regrown the cyst, I worry it's volatile and could possibly rupture if she's forced to endure any kind of stress."

That sounded life-threatening. "I'll hold off until then," I said. "But the moment I hear from you, we're leaving."

"I'll be in touch as soon as the test results are in," she said. "Again, my apologies. I had vetted the program through two other colleagues, but I should have done so myself. I'm in contact with them now and I'm alerting them to the state of this situation. As I am the state medical board. I assure you, if there is anything untoward happening in the program, the right people will soon know about it."

That was reassuring. "Hopefully the scan is clear, and she'll improve once she's home."

Dr. Jessup hesitated. "If the scan is clear," she said softly, "I'm far more concerned, Ms. Pringle. Though a rapid regrowth doesn't bode well, if there's permanent damage to her brain, it may require much more invasive surgery and therapies to repair the problem. If we can."

I didn't want to hear that but accepted it. "Thank you for calling back," I said. "I'll be here with Thalia the whole time, so whatever you learn, I'm present to deal with it."

She said her goodbyes and hung up while I turned my back on the three lovely souls playing with plants and had a solid moment of grief over what could be before jerking myself under control. The tears I'd let silently slip were quickly dashed away with both hands, my wave of emotion crested and released and the future again just a ream of possible outcomes instead of the dread-filled and weighty terror of what I feared was coming.

Thalia thought she and the rest of the Vesterville family were cursed. I really hoped she was wrong.

By the time I rejoined the girls, Thalia was fading, though she seemed more herself. I returned Belladonna to her carrier while Calliope helped her girlfriend up the stairs and through the door. She was barely seated in the waiting wheelchair when someone came hurrying down the steps and joined us. He beamed a lovely smile, hazel eyes behind his glasses taking in the three of us while he offered his hand to me.

"Gray Fender," he said, lean and short and a bundle of energy I could feel as he firmly but kindly shook my hand. "I'm one of the interns. Dr. Yonan asked me to make sure Thalia was taken care of."

I just bet he did, though taking out my grumbling

anger on the intern wasn't going to help. "Thank you," I said. "We're waiting on an MRI?"

He bobbed a nod. "The technician isn't in right now," he said, taking over from Callie and pushing Thalia down the hall, "but he's been called in so we're hoping he'll be here tonight."

"I'll chat with Dr. Yonan about the urgency of this test," I said, not meaning to sound ominous but knowing it came out that way.

"Oh, he knows," Gray laughed, using one hip to open the door to the residences, spinning Thalia expertly in her chair to accomplish it. I followed, Calliope beside me, Belladonna silent in her carrier for once. "Trust me, the whole facility is in a state since your arrival." He winked at me with that smile still in evidence. "Thanks for that."

"How long have you worked here?" I wasn't sure how to take him and as he turned around again, now in the residential corridor, he carried on speaking but in a lower voice.

"Just six months," he said. "It's a job." He shrugged but his good humor didn't fade. "Thalia's one of my favorites, right, Thalia?"

She smiled up at him, nodding. "Thanks, Gray."

"My pleasure." He paused at Thalia's door, letting Calliope go ahead of us, taking her girlfriend inside while Gray leaned into me with his smile fading a little. "I do my best to watch out for her, but the truth is, Asher Wyatt is a problem, Ms. Pringle, and I'm not the only one who knows it."

And yet, no one did a thing to stop it. "Thank you, Gray," I said. "Let me know when the technician arrives?"

"You got it." He saluted me and then the girls inside. "I'd offer to get you back to bed, Thalia, but it looks like you're in great hands." He turned back to me again, barely my height, hazel eyes on level with mine. "Unless you want me to take care of it?"

It was actually nice of him to ask, and I felt relieved at least someone had a heart in this place. "We've got it," I said. "Thanks again."

"Anything for Thalia." He spun and marched off. I watched him go a moment before entering the room and closing the door. By then, Calliope had parked Thalia's wheelchair and was helping her into bed. I hurried to assist from the other side, depositing Belladonna's carrier on Thalia's feet, though it was clear to me the Vesterville heiress had shaken off some of whatever drug Dr. Yonan had given her and was more herself at last.

"Thank you," she said, patting her lap when I unzipped the carrier again. It took Belladonna a minute to emerge, but when she did, she went right to Thalia, her engine firing up and purr rumbling through the room. "I don't know what's gotten into me lately."

I cleared my throat so neither of my girls would hear the thickening in my voice when I spoke. "As soon as your MRI is done, we're out of here," I said.

Thalia perked at that, as did Calliope. But when Thalia sagged, I knew what she was thinking. "I can't go back to Vesterville House," she said.

"You're not," Calliope said. "You're coming home with us."

Thalia looked back and forth between us, shock on her face. "I wouldn't want to impose on you, Seph."

I bent and hugged her, my gaze locked with Callie's. "You could never," I said, finally losing it a little, knowing my voice cracked and warbled and my breath hitched. "Thalia, I should never have let you come here. So, I'm correcting that. You're going to stay at my house, both of you, until you're better and can make a decision about what you want to do next."

She wept as she hugged me back, Calliope embracing both of us, Belladonna meowing and head-butting all of us for attention. I pulled away finally, reaching for a tissue, while the girls talked in happy voices and my cat purred.

I couldn't join them as much as I wanted to. Because while I'd just given them both hope, there was none left over for me. I may have just agreed to let the young woman die in my house.

And, if so? So be it. One thing was certain. There was something rotten about this place and I couldn't trust Dr. Yonan or his objectivity when it came to Thalia. If taking her home was the last place she went, I was all in.

I'd deal with the heartbreak that followed if the time came.

CHAPTER EIGHT

I wasn't happy to see Jose appear, especially with another tray of syringes in hand, but when I questioned him, he grudgingly admitted it was a simple blood taking. I'd assumed he was an orderly, not a nurse, and pushed him on the matter.

"I'm an RN," he said somewhat stiffly and with resentment in his eyes and voice. I wasn't making friends, apparently, but I didn't really care. Thalia had to be my primary concern. Knowing he wasn't happy had me contemplating calling for another nurse, but Jose dove in before I could stop him.

Fine, carry on. But hovering over him and keeping an eagle eye on his technique was the price he paid. At least he didn't complain on that end, doing his job diligently and without further drama.

No, the drama was all mine, in my head, swirling worry and lingering anger making me restless. And while I figured it was part of Dr. Jessup's requirements for the pending MRI, I was still loathed to let anyone in the facility have control over Thalia in any way.

When he was done drawing blood (gently enough, so I had no reason to complain), I immediately took possession of the tray before he could do a thing about it.

"Dr. Yonan won't like it," he grumbled.

"Dr. Yonan can suck it," I said. Okay, I didn't say that out loud. I wanted to, believe it. Instead, I said, "Ms. Vesterville's care is under my purview."

Jose grunted then shrugged and left without further comment, so score a win for the home team. Callie and Thalia had both remained quiet during the exchange, the uncomfortable silence only punctured by Belladonna's comforting purrs that kept the whole situation from spiraling into a puddle of anxiety.

"I'm going to take this to the lab personally," I said, the girls just nodding, heads together, my cat between them. "Callie, if anyone tries anything, you call me immediately."

My daughter nodded before hugging her girlfriend a little tighter. "I got this, Mom," she said. "No one's getting near Thalia from now on."

She had enough of me in her to balance out her father, didn't she? Which meant I was free to carry on without too much concern, though lingering doubts remained, and I was more than eager to hand over the blood work to the lab and get back to the girls before something else traumatized Thalia.

This time the security guard didn't give me trouble, instead dispensing directions when I asked for the lab. He sent me down the hall under the OFFICES sign and to the right at the T, the glass window open and a young woman on the other side in a white lab coat looking up when I set the tray on the ledge between us.

"Thalia Vesterville," I said.

The brunette nodded, light catching the lenses of her glasses, kind enough smile flashing before she took the tray in hand. I'm not too proud to admit I held onto it a bit longer than was necessary, her startled expression at the struggle to liberate it into her control making her pause and meet my eyes again.

"Sorry," I said. "I'm concerned about her care."

She bobbed a nod without any sort of resentment. "I'll process her bloodwork personally, Ms...?"

"Pringle," I said. "Persephone."

"I assure you I'll take the best care of Ms. Vesterville's labs, Ms. Pringle." Her attitude hadn't shifted from that kind and caring professionalism she'd shared from the get-go, so I released the tray and stepped back with a short exhale.

"Thank you." I was surprised by my level of anxiety. "Dr. Sandra Jessup is waiting for the results."

"I have her on file for Ms. Vesterville." She nodded again. Either the tech had excellent recall, or she'd already been alerted to Thalia's case. More than likely the latter. Which meant Dr. Yonan was taking this seriously, at least. Probably to make sure he covered his own butt, sure, but if it meant Thalia finally got the care she needed, I'd take it.

And his license.

Snarl.

I strode past the other corridor leading to the offices, not in the right state of mind to have another clash with Dr. Yonan. And honestly, everything I needed to say could wait until Thalia was on the mend. If she was ever able to mend. I mentally shook myself because I couldn't think that way, right? Except it was so hard not to linger in doubt and worry while in this place.

Vesterville House and its looming curse had nothing on this place. It felt like walking through the physical representation of impending doom.

I was passing the lobby and heading for the residence corridor when my phone buzzed. Is it wrong my heart thudded in terror something horrible happened? If Thalia had taken a turn or there had been a disaster while I was playing at protecting her, I'd never forgive myself.

I dabbed at the sweat that beaded my upper lip in response to the text only to exhale a shaking sigh at the words Calliope sent me.

Thalia wants her plants. We're in the greenhouse. She seems calmer.

Okay, Seph, enough with the panic attacks. *On my way.*

By the time I reached the door and the stairs, I'd

regained my composure and even managed a smile as I descended to the greenhouse proper, the small space feeling much lighter than the oppression of the expensively appointed and yet overbearing building behind me. Thalia was laughing, holding up the aloe plant to Callie who shook her head, both hands out.

"You know I have a black thumb, Lia," my daughter said. "If you want the thing to keel over, hand it here."

Thalia giggled and set it aside. "You just haven't given it a real try, Callie."

"Oh, I beg to differ." I joined them with my smile widening. Thalia truly seemed composed and brighter, as though some dark cloud had passed over her. Had I been overreacting? Was she really only in need of my daughter's company, my cat's? And mine, dare I say? Belladonna turned over in the dirt on the surface of the table, her white fur speckled with dark bits I'd be brushing out for days, I was sure, though she seemed delighted by the chance to enjoy the fresh soil. When I'd adopted her, she'd been an outdoor cat for the first year of her life, something she still longed for if her almost magical escapes meant anything. And though I'd given her a nicely fenced and safe space in my own yard for her to wander, I knew how much she loved the freedom of just being a cat.

"Mom," Callie eye-rolled as she dragged out that word. "You promised."

Thalia looked back and forth between us, eyes alight for the first time since her surgery. No, since well before that, truth be told, the tumor's influence going back months. "What? Seph, no secrets."

I grinned and booped my daughter on the end of her button nose. "This one begged for an orchid when she was six," I said. "Just before she met you, actually, Thalia." Calliope groaned and tossed her hands, though light-hearted enough I knew she wasn't against this attempt to augment Thalia's mood.

"It was so pretty," Callie said. "All pink and white and tall. I thought it was a fairy sleeping."

Thalia exhaled, one thin hip against the table, dreamy expression soft. "I know what you mean," she said. "I love that about orchids." She snapped back as she looked to me then her girlfriend with growing mock horror. "Oh, dear. What happened?"

"It didn't go well." Callie's wince had Thalia laughing.

"You could say that," I said. "She decided if the fairy was going to actually hatch or whatever her little mind contrived, it needed nature and the outdoors. So, she took it outside and planted it in the garden."

"That's a lovely sentiment," Thalia said, one hand reaching out to Calliope to squeeze her fingers.

"In January," Callie said.

Thalia's gasp of horror was followed by the two of them pealing with laughter. Belladonna leaped to her feet at the sound, shaking off the dirt she'd accumulated, almost offended by the loudness, especially when I joined in. The pure joy of it was contagious regardless and I suddenly felt so much better about the outcome of this particular situation. Whatever happened, we had Thalia back and I wasn't about to let her go again.

When our amusement died to the occasional chuckle, Thalia let out a long, slow breath, entire body sagging a little as she did, but not in defeat. If anything, she shone brighter than she had in ages and when she met my eyes, hers were soft and full of hope.

"Thank you for coming," she said. "I'm so sorry for how I've been behaving." Callie tried to hush her with a hug, but Thalia shook her head, kissing her softly on the cheek. "I've been beastly, and yes, I had good reason. But I'm still sorry. It's not like me." A faint frown pulled her thin brows together slightly. "I'm feeling so much more myself with you two here. And knowing I'm leaving this place, it helps a lot. It's just sometimes I feel myself, like now. And others... I just can't keep it together. As if there's a fog or something that falls over me." The psychedelics? Or anti-depressants? Probably both. I fought off the surge of resentment toward Yonan, wanting to stay in this lovely bubble of happy with my girls for as long as I could, if only for Thalia's sake.

"We're just happy you're going to be okay," Calliope said. "Right, Mom?"

I nodded without speaking because I was not about to burst the thin veneer of hope hanging around us, thanks.

Thalia's expression firmed up, determination crossing her gaze. "I've decided I'm not going back to Vesterville House," she said. "As soon as I'm well, I'm going to either sell it or at the very least close it up for good."

An excellent idea for her mental health. "Whatever you decide," I said, "I know it will be the right choice for you, Thalia." It was just a pile of rocks with a horrible history, after all. I wasn't the most sentimental person I knew, however, so I hoped she wouldn't regret it down the road. Then again, she had more than enough money to make a life for herself anywhere she chose, so strapping herself down to a place that held nothing but negative memories for her boded ill for her future.

We spent the rest of the morning in the greenhouse, Thalia's condition so improved I felt comfortable leaving them long enough to fetch lunch. Truth be told, I needed the physical outlet the walk gave me at that point to shake off my impatience, returning with an orderly who insisted on assisting, one of the servers from the kitchen joining him to set up a nice little picnic for us, table, chairs, tablecloth and all. Again with the five-star hotel service, but this time I wasn't complaining. It was a comfortable temperature in the greenhouse and Thalia's mood had improved so dramatically under the influence of her plants I had no issue staying there for the duration if that was what it took.

I finally stood from the table long after we'd finished and the settings were cleared, about to suggest I fetch a pair of blankets for the girls. They'd retreated to sit on the table amid the plants for a bit of privacy. Not that the coverings would be necessary, but it would give me something to do besides surf my phone and observe while Thalia and Calliope whispered together with Belladonna between them.

My cat perked suddenly as I rose, ears flattening and a low growl emerging from her while she backed away, tucking herself behind Calliope. Startled by her sudden reaction, it was enough warning to get me into motion.

The cracking sound still behind me caught me by surprise, though Belladonna's following yowl had me moving faster, her protest preceding the sound of glass shattering just enough I was able to leap forward and grab my girls. I pulled them close with my head down, Belladonna leaped to the ground at my feet, hiding under the table while the panel of glass behind me burst inward. I was thankful I hadn't shed my coat, shards impacting my back, the pattering fall of slivers on the ground punctuated by horrible laughter that had me turning around with a scowl.

Asher Wyatt sat in his wheelchair on the other side of the greenhouse frame, a rock in one hand. I looked down to find another at my feet, the one he'd used to break the panel in the first place so close it could have hurt me if it had made it any further. He bounced the second stone in his hand before tossing it to one side, and, with an arrogant head tilt, leaned forward.

But he didn't get to speak. Whatever it was he was going to say was lost in the shrieking fury that burst from Thalia's mouth. She was so fast in her lunging attempt to get to him I almost missed grabbing her, Calliope's quick thinking faster than mine, though even the two of us were barely able to contain the fury that emerged from the screaming Vesterville heiress.

I caught some of her words, most were incoherent again, the young woman who'd just been so level and steady and raised my hope to possibility again vanished as if she never existed, a raging animal in her place who, while thin and weak a moment before seemed possessed of boundless strength and the need for violence that left me shaking.

As did her final words to Asher that I made out clearly.

"If you come near me again," she raged, "I'll *kill* you!"

Asher laughed. That only fired up Thalia worse, of course, and had to have been his plan. I glared at him while I clung to the now weeping and struggling young woman beside me, while the quiet and shamed Nora appeared in a rush and began pushing Asher away, out of sight. Only when he'd vanished from view did Thalia sag as though all the energy had drained from her body, sobbing tearing her in two while I comforted her with soothing words that meant nothing in the face of this new incident.

Calliope and I exchanged looks, my daughter's terror renewed, and I hoped I hid mine because if I didn't, she'd know as clearly as I did that if something wasn't done, Thalia's story wasn't going to end well.

CHAPTER NINE

By the time we managed to get Thalia back to her room, word of what happened had spread sufficiently that Dr. Yonan made an appearance, Jose at his side and syringe in hand.

Thalia hadn't calmed completely, still mumbling and angry, fighting our attempts to get her into bed, pacing the room and releasing random outbursts that troubled me deeply. But when I turned at the doctor's arrival and realized what he intended, I put my foot down immediately.

"You're not sedating her," I said, putting myself between her and them, something that was feeling far too familiar already. "I can handle this. Drugs are not the answer."

Yonan's scowl of disapproval had my back up as

much as his lack of empathy. "We've experienced this over the course of her stay," he said. "I've attempted many therapies, Ms. Pringle." I took note of the dropped doctor and figured he'd discovered I wasn't who he'd thought I was. Which clearly gave him the courage to stand up to me, or the arrogance. Either way, his determination matched mine as we faced off in Thalia's room, Calliope doing her best to calm her girlfriend while I dealt with Dr. Do Little or Nothing. "The only way to calm her and protect her from herself is with medication and sedation."

"And I say no," I repeated. "I'm her primary therapist and have power of attorney. If you're looking for more legal action against you, Dr. Yonan, go ahead and try to stick that needle in Thalia's arm. I'll have you behind bars and this place shut down even faster than I anticipated."

I hated using legal threats, but there was no other recourse and Thalia's family lawyers would be thrilled to have something to do, I figured.

"She can't have her MRI in this state," he said. Oh, so he was going to try to bully me and hang the necessary test over my head, was he?

"I'll ensure she's quiet and still during the test," I said. Yes, I was shooting smoke out my ear, but if I was sure of anything it was that drugs weren't helping. I needed to understand what was going on with Thalia and the medications were just muddying the situation. It was part of the reason I'd chosen to become a holistic therapist and rejected psychiatry and more traditional treatments. I truly believed there were answers that didn't come in a bottle but in order to find them, I needed her off the medications they'd been pumping into her since her arrival.

His visible skepticism faded a little as Calliope finally convinced Thalia to sit, the young woman sinking to the edge of the bed. Belladonna crept to her and into her arms, Thalia hugging the cat and weeping quietly, body now sagging around the feline as the energy she'd managed to muster wore off.

"There," I said. "You see? She has to be allowed to process, Dr. Yonan." More disapproval, but I didn't care about what he thought at this point. "Now, are we ready for her MRI?" The intern, Gray, had mentioned a longer wait but I was just as happy not to have to spend another moment in this place. Clearly, my presence and Dr. Jessup's orders had made a difference.

He nodded reluctantly, lips twisting in a scowl. "The technician has arrived," he said. "I still suggest sedation to ensure her cooperation."

"And if I have to tell you one more time," I said, "we'll be walking out right now."

He grunted something I didn't hear, turning to gesture to Jose. The nurse left the room in his lumbering lope, Calliope guiding Thalia into the wheelchair she'd vacated not so long ago. When Yonan scowled at the cat in her lap, I waved him off with a flat expression.

"Therapy animal," I said. "Just try it."

The doctor's eyes snapped anger, but he backed off and led the way.

Look at me, more wins. Maybe things would turn

out all right after all.

I left Calliope in the hallway with Belladonna, reassuring her everything was going to be fine and personally wheeled Thalia into the room with the MRI. She'd settled sufficiently I hoped she'd be fine, and when she laid back on the bed and turned her head to look at me, I knew it.

"I'm sorry." She choked on those two words. "I don't know what got into me."

"It's not your fault," I whispered back, bending to kiss her forehead. "I've got you, Thalia. We just need this scan, okay? Are you going to be able to lie still?"

She nodded the barest amount. "It's like a monster lives in me," she whispered back. "Seph, what's wrong with me?"

I fought off more tears. She needed me to be strong for her right now. I squeezed her hands and tried a little smile, feeling my lips tremble. "We're going to find out," I said. "I'll be right in there." I turned and pointed at the room behind the glass where the technician waited. "If you need anything, just say my name and I'll be right back. Okay?"

Thalia nodded, wiping at tears escaping down her temples, but her brave little smile was the best part. "Thanks, Seph. I'll be fine."

I hated leaving her, but there was nothing to be done about it. It was the hardest few minutes of my life, I'm not ashamed to say, pacing in the small room while the technician ran the MRI, and the scans slowly came up on the computer monitors.

I leaned in immediately as they did, Dr. Yonan

hovering to one side, the young tech scanning the images right along with me. And while I wasn't a brain surgeon or trained to read MRIs, it was pretty clear to me that Thalia's scan was normal.

"She's healing well," the tech said to me, pointing at a location where once the tumor had lived. "No sign of recurrence."

Which meant whatever was going on with Thalia didn't have anything to do with the tumor. "You're sure there's no residual damage from the surgery?" Or the existence of the tumor in the first place.

"Not from what I can see," the tech said. "This scan shows only healthy brain tissue. Dr. Jessup did the surgery, right?" I nodded. "She's fantastic. Great job. Your patient is well on her way to full recovery."

I wanted to challenge him further, but he didn't seem to have an agenda of his own and even Dr. Yonan seemed relieved. Which had me scowling at the scans despite the good news because this wasn't good news at all.

What was wrong with Thalia?

"I'll have the scans sent to Dr. Jessup," Dr. Yonan said. Was that vindication in his voice? It better not have been. I spun on him with my disapproval of his irritating self-congratulation written all over my face. He had the good grace to pull back on his hubris, at least. "And her bloodwork when it's processed. Did you need anything else, *Ms. Pringle?*" He stressed the honorific, as though needing to one-up me in some way if not over the scans, the creep.

"Nothing," I said. "You've done more than

enough. The moment Dr. Jessup clears her for travel, I'll be taking Ms. Vesterville out of your facility."

Yeah, that went over well. "It's clear she's in need of further care," he said. "Removing her now would be foolhardy."

"Pumping her full of drugs is foolhardy." I tossed my hands and backed away from him, heading out the door to assist Thalia. "My decision is made, Dr. Yonan. Stay away from Thalia from now on."

Calliope curled up with Thalia on the bed once we'd returned safely to her room, the pair napping quietly with Belladonna between them. I impatiently awaited Dr. Jessup's call while pacing, unable to settle myself, and finally took a walk when Calliope opened her eyes and met mine.

"Mom," she whispered. "That's not helping."

She was right, of course. I couldn't sit still, so leaving was my only option. And I couldn't bring myself to walk the halls of the center, which meant I headed outside into the brisk November late afternoon, surprised to find the day had passed in drama and it was now fully dark at just before 5PM. The facility's distance from the nearby town meant the sky overhead was crystal clear and bright with stars, no competing light pollution in the way once I circled around the building and out of the glare from the front doors. I followed the path around the brick wall to the side gardens, now brown and quiet on the verge of winter, the brisk breeze chilly enough I tucked myself tighter into my coat. But my firm and fast walk kept me warm enough, the crackle of tree branches and patter of falling leaves from the oaks joining the sighing wind in the near silence of the evening air.

It helped to steady me and return me to a measure of calm, moments of anxiety prodding me with reminders of what was to come. I checked my phone several times, feeling it buzz at last, though not with a message from Dr. Jessup. Instead, it was a text from Richard Renfrew that had me pausing in my strides around the building, near the back corner of the property.

I'm so sorry to hear Thalia's care isn't working out, he sent. *I agree completely she needs to be off medications, especially if her MRI comes back clean. There's no way to diagnose her at this point without her being free of pharmaceutical interference. However, I don't doubt Dr. Yonan's methods, Seph. I've looked further into him, and his record is impeccable. If he deemed it necessary to sedate her for her own good, I trust him.*

My fingers trembled with the need to fire off a truly nasty reply. But Richard wasn't done.

I am concerned, however, that he did so without diagnosis, that he rushed to drugs before understanding the underlying causes. Okay, so not a total jerk. Seph, deep breath. Richard was trying to help. *If you need me to, I can fly out in the morning.*

I thought about it, considered it seriously. Then discarded the idea because as much as I liked and mostly respected him, Richard was still a traditional psychiatrist who chose meds over methods the majority of the time.

I'll keep you posted, I sent. *For now, I'm waiting on*

Jessup to release her so I can take her home. I'm hoping a less invasive treatment might give her time to heal emotionally and mentally as well as physically.

His reply had me sighing. *Not to armchair diagnose, Seph, but there's a good chance she might be bipolar.* I hadn't wanted to label Thalia, but her surges in emotion certainly felt like an imbalance. Still, that diagnosis didn't feel like a fit either, not with what I'd seen. Instead, it felt like some kind of mania, and until I could get her home and observe her in a more sedate setting without the influence of those who triggered her (looking at you, Asher Wyatt), it would be impossible to get a real read on her. *I'm here if you need me.*

I thanked him and exhaled mist into the cool night, leaning against the wall beside me a moment, letting the quiet and the darkness engulf me, feeling the weariness of the day's trials weigh me down and drain me to the point I yawned a jaw-cracking exhale. Maybe I was finally winding down. All of that emotional turmoil made it feel more like midnight than early evening. I hated the thought of leaving Thalia overnight in this place again, but perhaps it was the best choice? Get a fresh start in the morning? I briefly contemplated leaving Callie and going home to sleep and changed my mind instantly.

I could rest later. The sense of dread that settled over me at the thought of letting my girls stay at the facility alone shook me out of my moment of weakness and drove me forward to finish my walk, leading me to the rear of the building and the greenhouse. I stopped to glare at the broken pane of glass, now cleaned up and the hole covered in plastic, contemplating Asher Wyatt. And made a terrible decision I knew I'd learn to regret.

Time to have a little chat with the arrogant young man who made Thalia's life so miserable. And his wealthy parents be damned.

CHAPTER TEN

Rather than return all the way around the building now that I'd made my decision to confront Asher, I chose instead to return through the greenhouse, the back door unlocked. It wasn't until I entered the glassed space and headed for the steps, I realized I might be wasting my time because surely that entry would be locked this time of night. But nope, one more reason for concern about leaving Thalia here any longer than necessary. The rear door was wide open to the world.

Tsking over the fact (while now cold and grateful I didn't have to retrace my steps because I was contrary like that), I shivered as I pulled the door open and headed inside. I paused as I closed it behind me, slipping out of my gloves and blowing on my chilled hands, the sound of approaching voices silencing me. It wasn't the voices themselves that made me fall quiet and listen, but their matching tone of whispering conspiracy. Maybe I was in a heightened state of nosiness and maybe it was just my natural way of being, but regardless as the two people paused just out of sight on the stairwell to the basement level, their quiet conversation became audible.

"And I told *you*," the first voice said, angry and nasty, "your daddy can't help you here. As soon as that Vesterville waste of space is gone, I'm going to make sure you get lots of attention."

"Leave me alone, Asher." That was Luca, had to be. I crept forward and peeked over the railing, catching sight of a fully ambulatory Asher Wyatt, no wheelchair in sight, with the lovely young man who'd befriended Thalia pressed against the wall, the taller, heavier blond threatening the younger, slighter man. The stricken look on Luca's face had my blood boiling all over again, though before I could intervene, Luca firmly shoved Asher away and ran back down the steps, the scowling bully watching him go before turning to head my way.

I could have confronted him and almost did. That was the goal originally, after all. Except the sound of approaching feet had me second-guessing publicly arguing with a patient of the facility when I meant to do it privately. So, with my jaw set against saying anything unless it was on my terms, I nipped up the steps as quietly as I could and paused, waiting for Asher to encounter the newcomer with plans to follow him to his room after.

"You're late." Asher wasn't trying to keep his voice down this time, grumbling petulance only increasing my dislike of him.

"I came as soon as I could." Well now. I knew that voice, but what did Jose Delgato have to do with young Master Wyatt? "You know I have to be careful. I could lose my job."

"Whatever." Exactly like someone of Asher's ilk not to care even a little about the welfare of others. Then again, if Jose was up to no good and on Team Wyatt, he didn't deserve compassion. "Did you do what I wanted or not?"

"I did." Jose sounded sullen, unhappy. "They're going to find out if I keep it up, you know."

"That's your problem," Asher said. "Make sure she gets more before morning." His barking laugh had me frowning deeply. Who was he talking about and what was Jose to deliver? "They'll put her in the looney bin for sure."

Oh, he better *not* be talking about Thalia. Did he have something to do with what was wrong with her? Or was I jumping to conclusions and someone else in this place had something to worry about?

The only way to get an answer was to confront them and I wasn't prepared to do that. However, I was going to watch over Thalia like a hawk until we left this place. Just let someone try to tamper with her.

"Asher." A young woman's voice interrupted and I almost squeaked, jumping a little and risking a peek. Jose spun and headed back the way he'd come,

Nora meekly standing to one side with a wheelchair in her hands. Asher sat in it like a king taking his throne, nasty grin aimed at her while he did.

"Take me to my room, dog," he said.

He missed the flash of pure hate on her face, but I didn't. At the last moment, her gaze flickered upward, caught mine. In the instant I absorbed her newly acquired black eye and split lip, Nora registered surprise at my presence. Instead of revealing me, however, she smothered her shock instantly. She didn't out me though she had a clear opportunity, wheeling Asher away toward the residences while I slowly descended to the main floor and followed at a distance.

Maybe she was the target of Asher's little scheme? If he gave her that bruise and cut, things had escalated past bullying and into physical abuse. Surely, something could be done. It was clear he tormented and abused her, so whatever he had over her to control her had to be the source of the fury I'd seen. I held my distance, Nora making no indication she knew I was there or offering a warning to Asher I'd been watching and the two disappeared through the doorway to the main hall a moment before I pulled it open and looked out, holding back long enough to check where they went.

Turned out Asher's room was only two down from Thalia's on the other side of the corridor. As she pushed him through the door, Nora glanced my way one more time, a softly pleading expression telling me everything I needed to know.

The girl was in trouble, and no one was going to

help her if I didn't.

Assignment accepted.

Instead of disturbing the girls, I marched myself to the offices, waving off the security guard—a new one, the woman's gruff expression no match for my determined stride—and carried on to the branch in the hall, taking the left path this time. The space opened into a central reception area, the desk empty, though there were several doorways behind it, one of which was marked with Dr. Yonan's name. There was a light on in his office and I was about to approach when it opened and he emerged, not alone. The other visitor Thalia had that morning, Faith, was at his side.

And you better believe I ducked to the right and into the dark side hallway beside reception because my instincts weren't happy about what I was seeing. Sure, I could have been overreacting, but the distinctly personal and intimate way he hovered over her, how his head bent to hers and they talked in quiet voices? Wasn't the least bit professional.

I watched them pass, Dr. Yonan supporting her when they walked by, not noticing me. I almost followed, except as I moved to do so, a flicker of motion halted me. One of the other office doors slipped open and Gray Fender slid out. It was clear from the grin on his face he'd been eavesdropping and uncovered something that made him very happy. I held my breath as he hurried past, waiting longer than was comfortable for him to go before finally pursuing Dr. Yonan and Faith.

I didn't catch up with him until I was almost back

to Thalia's room, and this time instead of Faith, he stood talking with Asher. It was pretty clear from the slyly cruel look on the young man's face he had the doctor under his thumb, Yonan's discomfort visible in the tall man's rounded shoulders and stiff posture. Asher made a rude gesture at the doctor before spinning his chair around. He fumbled the move, however, as I recalled his pain from earlier, some damage to his wrist making him wince. But this was different, not a reaction to hurt, but more an overall lack of coordination. He swayed slightly as he righted himself, finally managing it and, weaving and wobbling somewhat, headed up the corridor. Dr. Yonan glared after him without attempting to stop him even when Asher's erratic journey almost ended in him running into a wall. While he didn't deserve my compassion, something seemed wrong, and I almost moved to help. Didn't, so you can judge me about that because I was judging myself, even as Asher finally exited around the corner and out of sight.

Okay, I was done being quiet and only observing. Time to have a serious talk with both Asher and Dr. Yonan, it seemed. Except, as I approached, drawing breath to deliver a scathing teardown, the door to Thalia's room opened and Callie emerged, Belladonna in her arms and a stricken expression on her face.

"I was just gone a minute," she said, panic audible as she looked up and down the hallway. "I had to use the bathroom."

"Thalia." Dr. Yonan spun to face us both, joining

us with concern and a soft touch for my daughter's shoulder a contrast to the demonized version of him I had been building since I arrived.

"We'll find her," he said, looking up at me, dark eyes serious. "This is why we sedate her, Ms. Pringle. Ms. Vesterville has a propensity for wandering off if she's not closely watched. It's one of the symptoms of her case."

"We'll have this discussion later," I snapped. "We need to find her before she hurts herself."

He nodded agreement, heading for the lobby. "I'll alert security."

I let him go, heart pounding, though I was pretty sure I knew where we'd find her. "The greenhouse."

Calliope hugged Belladonna tighter. "That's what I was thinking. Let's go."

We hurried, not running, but almost, my cat's unhappiness at our pace and her confinement in my daughter's embrace an echoing growl that trailed along with us all the way to the exit to the back hallway. I was just ahead of Callie, had my hand on the exit to the greenhouse proper, and pulled it open to let her through, when I was forced to halt behind her. She gasped, Belladonna leaping from her arms when my daughter's grip fell slack, hands thudding to her sides before both rose to cover her mouth.

I looked over her shoulder, panicked worry Thalia was injured, the only reason I could think of for Calliope's reaction, when I realized it wasn't the Vesterville heiress I had to worry about.

Oh, she was present, standing at the table in the dim light of the string of bulbs overhead, her focus on her plants as she hummed her happiness in tending them. Looked up and waved at us, beaming, oblivious or broken, I had no idea which. Because she ignored completely the crumpled form of Asher Wyatt lying at the bottom of the steps, his wheelchair tossed to one side like a toy amid the destruction of the pots lining the steps. From the odd and awkward angle of his neck and staring eyes I could just see the whites of, my conversation with him would never happen and nor would he be bullying anyone ever again.

Asher Wyatt was very dead, and it was very possible Thalia killed him.

CHAPTER ELEVEN

Was it wrong I found the handsome Major Crimes Unit homicide detective distractingly attractive while I tried to tell him everything I remembered about the events leading up to Asher Wyatt's death? Probably, but tell my hormones that. Don't judge me for being into tall, dark and handsome with sea-green eyes and a hint of silver at his temples, or the way he bent his head over mine with a serious, open expression, how the scent of him, while subtle, carried notes of coffee, vanilla and whatever fabric softener he used on his clothing, tied into the barest touch of his own pheromones that had me stumbling over my words and struggling to catch my breath.

"I know this isn't an easy situation," he said in a

deep tone a voiceover artist for Hollywood would envy, low and calm and gentle. "Do you need to take a minute?"

I shook my head, frustrated with myself, catching the gurney with the body bag exiting out the lobby doors, heading for the ambulance waiting outside. We'd retreated to the entrance of the facility to await the police after I'd herded the girls back into the building while making the 9-1-1 call. Yes, I alerted my good friend and our town sheriff in Wallace, Cherise King, about the predicament, but after I'd made the death known to the state authorities. She'd sighed over me finding yet another body—bless her heart for not commenting further—before telling me she'd make a call or two of her own.

Whether due to her intervention or the integrity of the Maine State Police, it hadn't taken long for two cars to arrive with an ambulance and van behind them, the coroner and forensics techs following the anxious security guard to the scene of the death while two uniforms went with, no doubt to cordon off the area. That left lean, towering and delicious to head our way, dark jeans and black boots hugging his muscular legs, midnight blue peacoat pulled up at the collar, one strong hand reaching for mine.

The fact he'd rather neatly ignored the spluttering and angry Dr. Amir Yonan wasn't lost on me as he introduced himself.

"Kellan Boone," he said. "You must be Persephone Pringle." I must? "Cherise King speaks highly of you," he told me while goosebumps rose on my skin and that close intimacy he created with his posture and presence locked me into my present predicament. With no end in sight, apparently.

"I'm usually more professional," I told him after partially spilling my guts. I hadn't expected him to be kind, or to offer a moment to collect myself without any apparent level of judgment. "But it's been a hard and emotional day for Thalia and my daughter."

"And yourself, no doubt." Boone nodded once, one hand hovering with pen aloft over his leather notebook. He'd taken copious dictation in a rapid hand while I'd meandered my way through what I knew and seemed more than attentive still. So, either Cherise had really made an impression, or he was just a good cop. Maybe both. Whatever the case, his attitude, while welcome from one perspective, wasn't helping when it came to keeping my cool. Not that I wanted him to be confrontational or dismissive, not in the least.

*Day*um, the man was delicious. And I needed to grow up already. Because I realized as I sorted through everything I'd said to him, his gentle quiet and sense of comradery had encouraged me to say things I might have held back from anyone but Cherise. Which meant either he was very good at his job, or I needed to vent some of my attraction energy before I said something I'd regret.

"Considering the circumstances," I finished with a flush, "there's an excellent chance it was just an accident. Asher could easily have fallen down the stairs."

"I'm afraid not." A short, stout man in round glasses with a salt-and-pepper mustache lurking over his upper lip had joined us without my noticing, looking rather ridiculous in contrast to the tall, stunning detective. White coveralls and blue booties were never a good look, the man's mustache twitching as he delivered the bad news.

"Hubbs," Boone said, nodding to me, "this is Persephone Pringle. Ms. Pringle, Dr. Niall Hubbard, my favorite ME."

The small man stuck his hand out, his large, warm hand firm. "So, you're the therapist detective, huh?" He laughed while I looked back and forth between them. "You're making quite the name for yourself, Ms. Pringle." He sighed then and shook his head, pulling off his glasses and squinting at them with watery, hazel eyes while he cleaned the lenses on the cuff of his coveralls. "I wish I had better news, Boone, but it's definitely foul play." He replaced his glasses, adjusting them as he went on. "I'll have to take a closer look at the morgue, but I noted a bruise forming on his neck with a ragged needle mark in the middle. Someone injected him with something hard enough to leave damage." My mind went to Asher's erratic exit after his conversation with Dr. Yonan while Dr. Hubbard went on. "The fall broke the kid's neck, no question, but was he already dead when he went down?" The ME shrugged. "I'll know more when I'm done with the autopsy."

"Thanks, Hubbs." Boone jotted new notes while the doctor turned to me again.

"Don't let this guy's good looks fool you," he said with a grin. "He's the best detective in the state.

Though, from the sound of things, you have a better track record than he does." He snorted before turning and walking off, waving back over his shoulder as he went, following the EMTs and techs as they exited the building.

Boone chuckled at the comment, lopsided smile so sexy I had to look away and take a breath, my hands firmly clenched in the pockets of my coat. What was wrong with me? Honestly, I'd sworn off dating anyone in law enforcement thanks to years with my ex. And I hadn't really had the opportunity outside a few truly terrible options to even flirt or think about finding someone to spend my life with. I was happy being alone after all those years in a relationship that never fulfilled me.

But now? Wow. Lust had come knocking and I really needed to rein it in. Thalia still needed me, Calliope, too. This was no time to let hormones turn me into a teenager with a hard-core crush on the hottest guy in school.

Oh, but he was *so* lovely to look at. I made a point of bringing up my last sight of Asher in reference to what the ME had said while Boone nodded and continued to write in his notebook. "I made the same connection," he said, but without a hint of irritation I might be interfering. In fact, as Dr. Yonan's protests became louder and the two officers who'd returned with the ME did their best to keep the man calm, Boone glanced his way before returning those gorgeous green eyes to me.

Why did I suddenly feel like I was all he could see?

CHAPTER TWELVE

"Frankly, I don't trust anyone who works here," Boone said, having nothing at all to do with my attraction for him, keeping it professional as I needed to. Yikes. "They have their own agendas. And while I know you do as well, I trust you and your track record, Ms. Pringle."

"Persephone," I said, wincing inwardly that it didn't come out as breathy as I thought it did. "Or Seph."

The detective smiled that little, sexy smile again. "Seph. Boone." He glanced at Yonan again while a hit of heat at the private moment warmed me up in places I needed to wrangle under solid control before I blurted something inappropriate. By the time he looked back, I had myself convinced I was solid and could handle this without embarrassing myself while knowing in my heart I was a horrible, horrible liar. "I'd like to ask you to join me during my interrogations. I could use the input of someone who's used to reading people."

"Is that permitted?" I almost kicked myself for trying to put myself out of the running to help out. I needed to be thinking about the girls, not spending more time with Detective Gorgeousness.

He seemed surprised by my question. "I guess you don't know," he said. "According to my bosses, you have certain privileges when it comes to working with us."

Huh. "I didn't know," I said, wondering just what it was Cherise had been telling other law enforcement about me but not about to shut him down. Especially if I could use this position to my advantage and help clear Thalia.

If she was innocent. Which she had to be.

"You do know I'm going to do everything I can to prove Thalia Vesterville had nothing to do with Asher's death." I wasn't going to let this animal attraction I felt for him get in the way of that.

He didn't seem put off by it in the least. "I have no doubt of that," Boone said. "But I can trust you to do the right thing no matter the outcome." That wasn't a question, those bottomless eyes devouring me while I swallowed and nodded.

"Of course," I said, sagging a little. "If Thalia did have something to do with Asher's death, I want to know, need to. She's not well, Boone." I glanced toward the corridor to the residences, Calliope and

Belladonna tucked away with Thalia in her room for now.

"So I understand." He slipped his pen and notebook into the inner pocket of his coat, revealing the dark blue button-up he wore beneath it, the sight of a belt buckle, a round, silver disk with a shining B in the middle flashier than I expected from him, taking my focus a moment. "I'm going to arrange for somewhere to talk with everyone you've mentioned. If you think of anyone else we should speak to, I'll add them to the list, but I'm confident you've been thorough, at least for the moment. I'll make my own assessment as we go." My phone rang as he finished, and he nodded to me as I held it up with a raised eyebrow. "Go ahead. Catch up with me when you're done." I watched him go as I thumbed the answer button, Cherise's face on the screen.

"How does he look?" Her question caught me off guard.

"What?" I blinked and turned away from my study of Boone's long stride and wide shoulders.

"The case, Seph. How does it look for Thalia?" Cherise sounded confused.

Whoops. Boy brain wasn't helping me at all. "Sorry," I exhaled, leaning against the security desk and trying to block out the sound of Boone speaking with the angry Yonan. The doctor's voice rose, "how dare you," the only three words I made out, while Boone's low rumble cut him off. "I'm not sure. The ME thinks Asher was drugged and could have been dead before he was pushed down the stairs."

"Would Thalia have had any access to something

to incapacitate him?" Cherise's focus was a huge boon (Boone? Oh, dear) because she pulled me out of my lingering attention on the detective and back to what really mattered.

"They've been sedating her and pumping her full of drugs, Cherise." I know my distress came through, the sheriff's low hiss angry.

"Listen," she said, "I hear Kellan Boone's on the case." News traveled fast. "He's a great investigator, talented and fair." She missed delicious and delectable, but I wasn't judging her. "He'll take what you tell him seriously."

"So I understand," I said, repeating Boone's deadpan line at her, letting wry amusement into my voice, grasping for the relief of stress in this chance to tease her. "I hear my name's making the rounds with the state police."

She chuckled. "You've proven time and again you've a nose for truth, Seph," she said. "And while I know we've had our disagreements when it comes to Thalia, you've always done the right thing by me and my department." In fact, we'd just come through one such disagreement, hadn't we, prior to Thalia's surgery? I knew we'd mended our particular fences, but it was heartening and touching to hear her say such nice things, even if I maybe didn't entirely deserve them. "Did he ask you for help?"

"In the interrogations," I said.

"Good," she said. "And." Her deep breath ended in a long exhale. "Seph, there's a chance he only asked you to do so because he wants to keep an eye on Thalia and getting on your good side ensures that."

I was an idiot. Of course, that had to be his tactic. Mind you, he'd been pretty upfront about things, so were we both overjudging him? Better to be aware, certainly. I turned to observe the detective who'd somehow managed to talk Dr. Yonan down to a calmer conversational tone. I didn't want to think ill of him, or that he was manipulating me, but he was a cop and uncovering the truth was his job. Honestly, her warning helped snap me out of my girlish attraction somewhat, if not completely, so I was grateful to a point.

"If Thalia was involved," I said, "she has to face the consequences, Cherise. But I honestly don't believe she has it in her to hurt someone else. If she did, it's only confirmation there's something terribly wrong with her."

"Fair enough," Cherise said. "Did you want me to drive up there? I can be there first thing."

I glanced at my phone screen, noted the time was now well past 7PM. "I'll call you in the morning if things are going wonky," I said. "Thanks, Cherise. For everything."

"I adore Thalia too," she said, voice cracking just a little. "And Callie. Hug them for me and send my love, okay?"

I hung up from the call with my throat thick with emotion, tucking my phone away and taking another second, head down, to pull myself together. The detective was waiting on me and I needed a clear head. But I had two things to do first.

One, an email to Juno, Morris and McCarthy to

alert Thalia's lawyers about the situation. And the second a text I hesitated over.

Someone's been murdered, Gaines. And Thalia is the prime suspect.

I hovered my thumb over the send button, before deleting the text and sighing. Let him be pissed I didn't tell him everything until after it was over. He didn't deserve to be in the know. With my chin rising and determination fueling my heart, I turned and crossed to Boone to do what I could to make sure the truth proved Thalia innocent.

Or not.

CHAPTER THIRTEEN

It was strange to sit down with Boone at the small table in the cafeteria. Sorry, dining room, equipped with nicer cutlery and tablecloths than I had in my own house. I shed my coat, Boone taking it from me and laying it over the back of my seat, though he didn't offer to pull my chair out, for which I was grateful. So, a gentleman but also conscious of my independence?

The fact he wasn't wearing a wedding ring had zero bearing on my encroaching increase of interest, I swear it.

The detective divested himself of his peacoat, draping it across the side of the table, crisp navy cotton button-up a perfect fit for him, that belt-buckle catching my eye again. As did his strong jaw with a hint of stubble, the crinkling around his eyes and full mouth and how his big hands cradled the pen and notebook with a care of attention that had me wondering what other talents they possessed.

Oh, Seph, come *on*, for pity's sake.

Dr. Yonan, for his part, appeared immensely frazzled as compared to when I'd seen him earlier. Gone was his cool arrogance and composure. He'd run his hands through his hair one too many times for the waves to remain under control, a bit of a mad scientist look happening around his washed-out face, warm brown skin gone ashen and dark eyes now sunken as he fidgeted in the seat across from us, tie loosened and the knot askew, top button of his white shirt undone, and lab coat discarded. While it may have been an opportunity to get a bit of revenge on the man for what he'd put Thalia through, enough compassion remained within me I didn't revel in his visible distress.

Much. Hey, I was human, after all.

"You're here late, Dr. Yonan," Boone said, sitting back, crossing one leg over the other, casual tone and carriage meant to disarm, no doubt.

The doctor shrugged almost like a physical tic, shoulders jumping and hands flailing a moment in his lap before he licked his lips to respond.

"I had a patient to consult," he said, cheeks pinking under the gray of his anxiety. I just bet he did as my mind turned to Faith and their visit in his office. A visit I still suspected had nothing to do with her treatment. I realized then I'd failed to share that part of what I'd seen with Boone, only because it hadn't seemed connected to Asher's death. But was I wrong? I made a mental note to fill him in even as Yonan went on. "I was about to leave when we realized Ms. Vesterville was missing." His gaze flickered to me, that scowl returning. Like he blamed me for Asher Wyatt dying or something. Or, at the very least, Thalia. He could take that look and stuff it. "A tragic circumstance, just tragic."

"I understand the Wyatts are in India?" Boone looked up from his notes, still with that casual and caring tone, expression open, almost kind.

"Indeed," Yonan said, sitting forward and then back, a man uncomfortable in his own skin. "I have been unable to reach them, but I will continue to attempt to do so. Until then, the family's lawyers are their only contact." He sounded like that was the last option on his list, blinking rapidly and swallowing so hard his Adam's apple bobbed with aggressive force over the collar of his shirt and into his short, dark beard.

I glanced up as motion to my right caught my attention, the door to the dining hall blocked with several figures, the uniforms keeping them back but their faces familiar enough. Faith's distress seemed the most obvious to me, Luca's frown and Nora's hard stare at the floor not unexpected. I was surprised they'd been assembled like this, observing Dr. Yonan's interrogation, while Thalia and Calliope remained in her room. Made me wonder about the detective's tactics, and if he only sequestered the Vesterville heiress because he believed her guilty.

"Were you aware Mr. Wyatt was having

difficulties with other patients, Dr. Yonan?" Boone's question brought me back to the table and the now spluttering psychiatrist.

"I assure you," he snapped at last, "whatever this woman told you," his index finger shook as he jabbed it in my direction, "is an outright falsehood. Mr. Wyatt's parents entrusted his care to me, as do the families of all my patients. While he might have been struggling emotionally with his injuries and recovery, Mr. Wyatt certainly didn't bring on his own death, if that's what you're implying."

Boone's faint smile had me curious. "Interesting," he said then, ever so quietly, while Dr. Yonan flinched. When Boone didn't say another word for a long moment, the psychiatrist paled further.

"I had nothing to do with his murder," he blurted.

Boone didn't move or change tone, but his words chilled me to the bone. "We don't know Mr. Wyatt was murdered, Dr. Yonan."

The doctor's lips parted, and he stared at the detective, wild-eyed and trembling, before sagging in his seat. "I only assumed," he said, one hand rising to run over his face, the rasp of stubble on skin loud in the quiet.

"We're still investigating." Boone closed his book, glancing at the group at the door before waving at the officers. To my surprise, the pair led the waiting watchers away and it wasn't long before we were alone with Dr. Yonan. Only Faith seemed reluctant to go, but even she finally obeyed. All of which Boone observed with quiet eyes and no change of expression.

When he finally returned his attention to Dr. Yonan, he smiled, leaning forward to shake the man's hand. Yonan returned the gesture with a dazed expression, half-rising while Boone surged to his feet and motioned to the door.

"I realize you must be in a state of shock," the detective said, leading the doctor to the exit, one of the uniforms appearing and nodding her head to her boss. "Please escort Dr. Yonan somewhere he can sit and rest. But don't go home just yet." He patted the man gently on the back before turning and rejoining me, Yonan glancing over his shoulder at us as Boone sat on the table beside me, leaning in.

"You're a terrible person," I said, finally getting it.

Boone winked. "You judge me too harshly, Seph."

"Do I?" I shook my head, though I couldn't keep the grin from my face. "I see it now, what you're up to. Let the others watch you talk to the doctor, but far enough away they can't hear what's being said. Then send them off with more questions than answers while you let the doctor feel like he's done. Except he's far from done and he's trapped here like a rat. He'll spend the next however long you give him to stew in his own juices digging a grave for himself."

Boone tapped the tip of his own nose with one finger. "They warned me you were clever."

"That means you left Thalia in her room for a reason," I said, all admiration aside. "You really do think she did it."

Boone sighed, staring down at his hands in his lap, the silver buckle's shiny B winking at me behind them. "I hate to say it, but she's the most viable suspect, Seph. Hear me out." I crossed my arms over my chest while he took in my reticence then went on in that same reasonable tone I knew was going to rankle in short order, gorgeous face or not. "The victim had been bullying her since she arrived." He ticked off one point on his index finger before going on. "She's not been herself." I had to give him that as the second finger fell. "His attack on her sacred space this afternoon triggered a death threat." Hey, those were just words, mister, but yeah. Okay then. Drop that finger, why don't you. "And she was found with him in the greenhouse after his death."

"You're forgetting the bruise and possible injection," I said.

"I'm not," he said, pinky falling. "She had a history of sedation and could possibly have managed to get her hands on a dose." He blew out a breath then, sitting back, shaking his head before I could argue. "Yeah, that's a dumb one. Unless she had help." He fixed me with those green eyes.

Oh no, he did *not* just accuse me of something. He was less and less attractive by the... never mind. Still gorgeous. Besides the point, though. "If you think I dosed Asher Wyatt, you've cracked your fine-looking noggin, detective."

He grinned suddenly, arms crossed, expression almost boyish. "I had to at least throw it out there. Okay, you're off the hook. And you're right about the drug. But if he was attacked and dosed, there's still a chance Ms. Vesterville had an altercation with him and pushed him down the stairs."

"Or, more likely," I said, "he was there to torment her, was high as a kite from the jab, and tried to roll his own sorry butt down there to do more damage and ended up killing himself."

Boone contemplated it, shrugged. "Let's see what Hubbs has to say," he said, "but that's as viable a scenario as any. Which means we're also looking for someone with access to injectable drugs."

My phone buzzed, the sight of Callie on the screen making me tense and sit forward. I'd gotten rather comfortable being there, talking with Boone and had forgotten my girls were alone.

Mom, I need you.

CHAPTER FOURTEEN

I stood immediately, leaving my coat behind, Boone joining me next to the table. He was far too close for comfort, only an inch or so between us, and hovered there, concerned look on his face, until he finally cleared his throat and took a firm half-step back, green eyes shadowed.

"I have things to look into," he said. "I'll come find you when I need you again."

I hurried away, the weird mix of emotional stirrings and physical ones warring with my worry for the girls all the way to Thalia's door. When I arrived, fearing the worst (and imagining what that worst might be) I instead found them huddled in her bed with the cat in their laps, both of them pale and miserable while Belladonna chirped her concern at me.

Thalia burst into tears when I appeared, holding her arms out and I went right to her, scooting her over so I could sit on the other side of her bed. Good thing this was no ordinary hospital, the queen-sized big enough for the three of us to snuggle while Belladonna's purr fired up one more time while Thalia wept on my shoulder.

Calliope's eyes were as red as her girlfriend's, so they'd both been crying since I parted ways with them, wrenching my heart with the depth of her despair. When Thalia finally pulled away, I reached for the box of tissues someone tossed on her legs and handed her a few, took two for Callie and helped myself to some, the three of us blowing our noses and dabbing our eyes to the counterpoint of Belladonna's comforting rumble.

"Thalia," I finally said, "do you remember what happened?"

She didn't answer right away, head falling back, eyes half-closed, weariness written all over her face. But she did manage to speak despite her now verge of sleep. "It's all hazy," she said. "Did he hurt my plants?" She wept silently then, face contorting with it, but not a sound emerging as I wiped her face with a fresh tissue and sadly met my daughter's eyes.

"What did the cops say?" Calliope whispered that question, Thalia's breathing steadying as she quietly passed out, snoring softly in my arms.

"They're investigating," I said, leaving it at that. "You said you went to the bathroom?"

Callie sighed deeply, running her fingers through

Thalia's hair, straightening it away from her face, tender expression deeply hurt, lower lip between her teeth. "I thought she was asleep," she said. "I shouldn't have left her." She burst into her own tears, forcing me to lean in and hug both girls, the conscious and the still sleeping, while my cat shuffled positions to keep from being squashed.

"It's not your fault," I said, kissing her forehead. "Callie, if anyone, it's mine. I should have insisted we leave the moment I realized Thalia wasn't getting better."

"You did your best, Mom," Calliope said, pulling back and tearing a tissue to shreds before helping herself to a fresh one, the remains piling up with the used ones between Thalia's knees. It was a sad little mountain of white we'd built and wasn't going to get smaller by any means.

Someone knocked on the door, Callie calling for them to enter, though the sight of Detective Boone had her frowning. But he only waved a little, concern and compassion in his expression, voice low and deep when he spoke.

"I only wanted to check in on Ms. Vesterville and yourself, Ms. Pringle."

"Garret," she corrected him, slouching back.

"Ah," he said. "My apologies. You've been through an ordeal, and not the first time, from what I understand. You and your mother have a bit of a history with this kind of thing."

"So does Thalia," Calliope snapped at him.

To Boone's credit, he didn't take offense, both hands raised in front of him, a sign of surrender and a plea for calm. "I'm not here to arrest anyone, Ms. Garret. I only want to find out what happened so your friend can move on from this and get whatever help she needs."

"My *girl*friend," Calliope said, biting off that last word with real venom. "Detective."

Oh, dear.

"Callie," I said, low and firm. She shot me a look of rebellion but sniffed and tossed her head rather than argue. "You'll forgive my daughter for her rudeness, Boone, because you're right. They've both suffered horribly, and not just here." Callie's lower lip trembled but her jaw firmed. I knew the last thing she wanted was to cry or show vulnerability in front of him, so I didn't reach out to squeeze her hand. "Did you need something from me right now?"

"I can wait," he said. "And will, until Ms. Vesterville is able to talk." To my surprise Belladonna stood and stretched, her purr morphing into a series of chirps aimed at the detective. When he smiled and held out his hand, she strolled to the foot of the bed and head-butted his fingers. The fact Boone seemed to know just where to scratch won her over immediately, her purr returning as she dropped all of her weight into his hand and rolled over with her paws curled against her chest.

"She's beautiful," he said.

"Belladonna is a registered therapy cat," I said. "She usually goes to whoever needs her the most." I met his eyes as he looked up in surprise, noted his grin fading and wondered then what it was about him that triggered the cat's attraction. Or maybe it wasn't just me.

From the flicker of darkness that crossed his gaze, I'd seen more than he'd planned. Boone cleared his throat and backed away with one last pat for Belladonna. She yawned and growled a little complaint before returning to Thalia's knees where she settled to watch him with her own glowing, green eyes.

"Whenever you're ready, Seph," he said, gaze troubled a moment before he nodded and left. Calliope turned to me, fierce scowl fixed, and teeth clenched.

"What is he talking about?"

I hadn't anticipated her opposition. "I'm helping the detective with the case," I said. "Callie, this is a good thing." She inhaled to argue, and I cut her off with a squeeze of her wrist, safe now that he was gone. "I'm here for Thalia 100%. You know that. I've proved it many times." Her face crumpled and she nodded, her antagonism vanishing. I knew it was only a reaction to her own trauma and her worry about Thalia, but it was something we'd have to tackle at some point, even if I had to send her to another therapist to do it. "It's better this way. I'll make sure the truth comes out."

Calliope hugged me then, settling back with Belladonna and Thalia. "I don't trust cops."

"Your father's in that line of business," I reminded her as I stood and straightened my clothing. Did not look in the mirror to check myself out. Did *not*. Sigh, okay, I did. Vain much?

"Dad's not exactly the most trusted person on

my list right now," she grumbled.

I wasn't going to argue Trent's recent behavior with her, however, I also always promised myself I'd never speak ill of him in her presence because our divorce had been hard enough on her as it was, and she deserved a good relationship with him. That was if he was willing to put the work in. Which he hadn't been lately.

Or most of her life, truth be told. Grumble.

"I love you," I said, waiting until she grudgingly met my eyes before going on, "and so does your dad. No matter what happens, Calliope, you *are* loved. I hope you know that."

She was crying again, but her expression had softened. She waved me off when I circled to hug her. Like that was going to work. And if she didn't want my embrace, why did she cling to me for so long and so hard?

When she finally let me go, I kissed her softly on the forehead like I used to when was little and pulled a blanket up around the two young women I loved so much, pausing to give Belladonna some scratches before leaving them to one another.

I was tired, bone-weary by now, but rest could wait. I had a possible murder—assault at the very least—to solve and no way was I falling down on the job if I could do something to protect the love on the other side of Thalia's door.

CHAPTER FIFTEEN

Boone sat far too close to me as we huddled in front of the monitors at the security desk reviewing the footage the detective had a rushed warrant for. Dr. Yonan's continuing protests only made my companion and sort-of partner all the more relaxed and benign, as though conflict and pushback increased his ability to relax instead of making things worse.

I wished I had his poise, the combination of anxiety over Thalia and Calliope being alone tied into the worry I was a horrible person even considering the young woman I adored could have killed someone wrapped in a hideous worry I was actually right.

Oh, and the closeness of the divine man next to

me? Yeah, thanks for that added layer of stress, Universe. Being worked up and emotional while my hormones raged was exactly the way I wanted my night to go.

Though I wasn't completely focused, it didn't take a Ph.D. to figure out one of the cameras wasn't functioning properly and another had somehow lost a large chunk of time right around the death of Asher Wyatt. Boone didn't react to that fact, skimming through the footage while one of his uniforms stood by with the security guard to make sure she didn't tamper with what we were doing.

"There," I said, "that camera." Boone paused the filming, the image one I recognized as the entry to the back hallway. "There's nothing outside the back door to the greenhouse?"

He shook his head, pointing to the fuzzy screen. "According to our helpful friend over there," he nodded toward the guard whose visible discomfort had her shifting from one foot to another while dabbing at sweat beading on her forehead and upper lip, "that camera went out a few days ago and hasn't been fixed. And before you ask, the one near the exit by the stairs?" He flipped through that footage, the timestamp jumping by over an hour, showing Thalia, unfortunately, entering the greenhouse before the camera flickered and two EMTs appeared.

That was convenient.

Boone leaned back, fixing the guard with one of his easy, soft smiles. "Who has access to this desk?"

She shrugged, sweating harder, voice vibrating as she answered, her thin lips trembling, round cheeks glistening and pink. "Just me," she said rather sharply, cutting the words off in a harsh tone.

"Then you are responsible for the lost footage?" Boone rocked back in the chair, eyebrows raised, more chastising high school teacher for losing her homework than a homicide detective on the trail of a possible killer.

"No!" She shook her head, both hands up. "I had nothing to do with anything."

It was obvious to me she knew more than she was saying and before Boone could carry on with his reasonable questions, I interrupted. "Ms. Nanold," I said, reading her nametag, Connie Nanold visible over her heart on the dark blue uniform shirt she wore, "is there access to these cameras outside of this desk?"

She hesitated, glancing away to where Dr. Yonan paced and complained to the other uniform holding him back from interfering. The guard seemed to make a decision before sighing shakily. "Yes," she said, near to tears and with a hitch in her voice. "In the security office. Next to Dr. Yonan's."

Well, now.

Boone nodded sagely, not a glimmer of resentment for my intrusion appearing. "Thank you, Ms. Nanold," he said as he turned to me, lowering his already deep voice for only me to hear. "If Yonan threatened her, there's a good chance he's in on whatever happened."

"Or is trying to cover up the truth at the very least," I said. "Like evidence of Asher's treatment of other patients. If any of the bullying victims had footage to prove their stories," like Luca, for one, "the Wyatts would be in a sticky litigation situation."

"More than likely he's covering his bases," Boone agreed. "Let's see what we do have here before we question the doctor again." He gestured to the uniform standing guard over Connie Nanold. "Please secure the security office for me. I'll be there presently."

The uniform nodded to him, her eyes drifting to me a moment before she gestured for Connie to join her, depositing the security guard with her partner and Dr. Yonan then returned the way she'd come, striding down the corridor where the offices were found.

"You can't go in there!" Yonan's high-pitched complaint didn't earn him any points with me, and Boone ignored him.

"That's Asher," the detective said, pointing at the moment when the young man had wheeled his wobbly way from Dr. Yonan and headed to the corner.

"You see what I mean about his physical state," I said. "He must have been injected just prior to his talk with Yonan."

"But who did the injecting." Boone paused the footage and turned to the surveillance that had Thalia entering the greenhouse. I caught what he did with a soft exhale of relief. "Looks like she couldn't have been the culprit," he said. "She was already outside before Asher's conversation." He met my eyes. "How quickly would a sedative or injected medication take effect?"

"If it was a sedative? Fast," I said. I might not have finished my psychology Ph.D., but I studied drugs and interactions as part of my training. "Within moments, depending on the amount he received." I pointed to Asher's frozen form on the screen. "Likely he was injected just prior to his conversation and the drug was kicking in by the time he wheeled away."

"Why wouldn't he ask for help?" Boone frowned at the screen. "He must have known he'd been injected."

I shrugged, shaking my head. "Arrogance? Or he knew who drugged him and was pursuing them?" I pointed at the keyboard. "Rewind a little. See if anyone enters or leaves his room."

"My thought exactly." Boone did so. Except our joint idea didn't deliver the way we hoped, because it wasn't just one person who walked through and then out of Asher's door in the last few minutes before his encounter with Dr. Yonan. No less than five people paraded past the screen, including Luca, Nora, Jose Delgato, Gray and Faith. Each of them only lasted a moment, some of them crossing over one another, Jose arriving and leaving after Luca, for example. But it meant there was no clear winner when it came to suggesting who it might be that injected Asher.

I caught my breath as the last person paused at his door, my chest tight at the sight of Calliope hovering there, hand raised, though she never did knock. I caught sight of Thalia slipping away and down the hall while my daughter seemed to reconsider her choice to confront Asher. Callie looked up quickly and turned to hurry back to Thalia's room, going inside, just as Dr. Yonan appeared and Asher emerged alone to carry out their argument one more time.

"Is your daughter in the habit of lying to you, Seph?" Boone's gentle question had softness in it, but there was nothing soft about my reaction.

"She's been known to keep a few things to herself," I said, chest tight with anger. How could she? Gone to the bathroom, my butt. She'd been about to do something stupid and almost got caught and straight-up lied to my face about it. I thought we were past not telling each other the truth. Apparently, Calliope hadn't gotten the memo.

"It's clear whoever dosed Asher did so behind closed doors," Boone said.

"And since Thalia wasn't one of them," I said, "she's off the hook, right?"

He hesitated and then sighed, showing his latest glimmer of anything outside his relaxed detective who had it all together persona as surprising as his reaction to my question about Belladonna's attention. His eyes tightened around the edges, crinkling a little, something like sorrow on his face before he smothered it with a professional, steady stare.

"She might not have been behind his drugging," he said then, "but without video coverage, all we have is her word she didn't push him down the stairs."

"She was already in the greenhouse," I argued.

"If he'd come to torment her, it's possible she could have climbed back up and confronted him, pushed him and left him there, going back to what she was doing before you found her." I hated how reasonable and logical he sounded.

"No fingerprints?" Surely, they'd dusted the handles of the wheelchair. Would Thalia's show up?

"A few," he said, "but nothing to match Ms. Vesterville."

There was that much at least. "I guess we'll just have to wait to see if the drug or the fall killed Asher then," I countered.

There was that hesitation again. He shifted toward me, the chair he sat in pivoting as he leaned into me, full lips thinning in unhappiness. "I already know," he said. "Hubbs got back to me quickly. The drug might have incapacitated him, but Asher's neck was broken from the fall and he's confident that's what killed the victim. It was murder, Seph."

I inhaled slowly. "Or an accident." I wasn't losing hope yet, though it waned, I admit it. "Thalia was so out of it, Boone, it's more likely Asher opened the door and tried to get a rise out of her but was on the edge of unconsciousness and made a fatal error."

Boone thought about it, I'd give him that credit, before he nodded and sighed deeply. "I need to speak to Ms. Vesterville now," he said. And as nicely as he said it? He wasn't asking.

"What about the others?" I wasn't going to let him off the hook so easily or set him loose to go after Thalia without good cause. "Aren't you forgetting someone dosed the victim? What's to say they didn't follow him and push him to finish him off?"

"There is that possibility," he said.

"Might I suggest you allow me to talk to them without you?" He flashed a grin while I blushed a little, not just from his reaction but the zing of attraction his expression roused. "I'll tell them I'm working with you, of course, but they might be more willing to open up to me."

He paused long enough I almost spoke, only to have Boone seem to come to a decision, a wry smile cracking his handsome face. "Agreed," he said. Then, "Full disclosure."

"That's preferable if we're going to work together," I said stiffly back. Kind of tired of being lied to and manipulated by my own kid, let alone a gorgeous stranger whose scent and mere presence pushed my buttons.

"Luca Diaz," he said, voice dropping even further, so close to me now that I could make out the dark gray flecks in his green eyes. That's what made them seem so deep. "He's been on my radar since he arrived."

Luca? He seemed like such a nice kid. "What has he done?"

"It's not what he's done," Boone admitted. "His father, Marcus Diaz, runs a drug cartel out of Mexico City." Oh. Oh, dear. "Someone like Luca being the target of a bully like Asher Wyatt? Wouldn't sit well with Marcus. Weakness of any sort would be seen as reason for severe punishment."

"Why is Luca here?" I hadn't asked, hadn't thought it important.

"He's been sick since he was a child," Boone said. "At least, according to my DEA friend who alerted me to his presence here. Marcus only had one son, so he's had to tread lightly with Luca despite his disappointment." It wasn't the poor boy's fault. "It's been in the back of my mind if word reached Marcus that Luca wasn't standing up to Asher's bullying, he'd have ordered his son to take action to regain his family honor."

"Like murder," I said. Chilling and yet a way of life for some.

Boone sat back again, and I felt I missed the warmth he radiated, the air now cool and making me shiver. "All that being said, if you'll trust me to do so, let's eliminate Ms. Vesterville as a suspect, shall we? If Asher's original attacker did kill him—or his death was an accident," he didn't sound like he believed that for a minute and neither did I, really, "I'd rather get to the truth sooner than later." His lovely eyes held me locked in place. "Agreed?"

I nodded, naturally, because it was totally reasonable. And yet why did I get the feeling he still thought she was guilty?

CHAPTER SIXTEEN

I intended to start with Luca if only to uncover the truth about his history outside of Detective Boone's share. Not that I didn't trust Boone, but I liked to gain my own information and not jump to conclusions. Well, at least not without those conclusions being my own. I definitely had a propensity to jumping, but I preferred it happened on my personal biases and steam, thank you.

Instead, as the handsome detective took a call and left me to my devices, my choice to head back to Thalia's room for a quick check-in first meant I passed where Dr. Yonan had previously paced in obvious agitation, the officer who'd stood guard against his interrupting the investigation also missing. Wherever the good doctor (and I use that term lightly) ended up, hopefully, Boone would keep him from tampering with evidence any further.

Oh, you can believe I landed all of the accusations on Yonan for the missing footage. And, as a doctor, he'd know exactly where to jab someone and what to give him to knock him out. On the other hand, if Yonan had attacked Asher, why wouldn't the young man have called him out?

The mystery lingered, of course, and would until we figured out who dosed Asher and if he'd simply slipped or had been pushed. Either way, I had work to do and girls to check in on, and not a hint of sleep in sight.

As I passed one of the residences just before Thalia's room, I caught my feet slowing as my tired brain registered what I was hearing and reacted before I consciously caught the relevance of the voices I overheard through the partially open door. By the time I'd stopped and cocked my head to one side, staying out of the sight line of the crack, I again wondered if my concerns about Dr. Yonan and his relationship with Faith were valid.

"You can't say anything," Yonan was telling her, Faith just visible when I peeked through the opening and caught sight of her sitting up in bed, the doctor pacing back and forth across my line of sight. "I'll lose everything."

"It's going to be all right, Amir," Faith said, the familiarity of using his first name only increasing my concern. "Asher's parents will put a stop to any investigation once they get here. This will all be over soon and we—"

"Ms. Pringle." I spun in surprise, a grunt from the other side of the door and sudden silence making me scowl up at Jose Delgato. He towered over me, perpetual grimace feeling more threatening than usual as he loomed with accusation on his face.

"Jose," I said, straightening my shoulders while the door whipped open and Dr. Yonan's distressed glare joined his nurse's.

"Dr. Yonan," Jose said over me like I didn't exist, "the detective wants to talk to you again."

Yonan brushed past me, Jose trailing after him, the nurse glancing back at me with a deathly stare that did nothing to deter me and only fed my curiosity and determination. Because with a mug like that, access to all the meds and attitude for miles? Jose Delgato just jumped to the front of my personal list. I know, for no more reason than he annoyed me one too many times, but still, he fit, right?

It would bring me no end of satisfaction to dig in and find out what he was up to, even if it wasn't murder.

When I poked my head in the door, Thalia was asleep, Calliope snoozing beside her. Belladonna looked up and chirped a greeting, but settled down again a moment later when she realized I wasn't coming in. I let them rest, grateful Boone decided against waking Thalia to question her. Nothing would be served in disturbing her right now, I knew. She was in a fragile state and if she really didn't remember, lack of sleep and stress would only add to her issues. As I paced forward down the hall and found Luca's door, his name outside on a black placard in gold lettering, I paused. Calliope had been lying to me lately about things I wished she'd been honest about, something that troubled me deeply since I'd always believed we'd had an open relationship. What if Thalia had torn a page from my daughter's battered textbook and was choosing to keep me from the truth, too? What if they both were?

And didn't I say I didn't want to jump to conclusions? Right, these were mine, so that was okay. I just hoped Detective Boone didn't make the same mental leap I did. Which he surely had. Thus, my feeling he didn't believe Thalia.

My head hurt with all the maybes, could bes and unhappy connections I was making. Now who needed a therapist?

I knocked on Luca's door, relieved for the distraction, and was surprised when he answered almost immediately. He ushered me inside where I received a second shock, because he wasn't alone. Nora Teres sat on the small sofa under the window, her black eye and cut lip stark against her pale skin, the straight, blunt black haircut she'd chosen augmenting her pallor and fragile appearance. She started to stand, ashen face falling, dark gaze darting to Luca who gently waved at her to sit before joining her on the cushions.

"We have to talk to someone," he told her, cupping her hands in his. "Ms. Pringle is the best bet, Nora."

She didn't look at me, eyes locked on his, licking her cracked lips and shivering. But she didn't argue or try to leave so I carefully perched myself on the only remaining chair against the wall, close enough to them to create intimacy but not crowding them while I offered a small, sad smile.

"I know you must be so tired," I said. "I've forgotten you're both here to recover just like Thalia. This kind of stress isn't helpful when you're not well."

"I've spent a lifetime in the arms of my illness," Luca said without a hint of self-pity. "I have lupus," he said. His diagnosis surprised me as it most often impacted young women, but cases in males weren't impossible. "I know what you're thinking," he said then, lips twisting. "I'm not a *girl*." There were underlying psychological issues there, clearly, his bitterness unmasked. "Trust me, my father makes sure to remind me just how feminine this disease is meant to be and that having it means I'm weak." Boone's assessment of Marcus Diaz was obviously correct if he bullied his own and only son about being sick, something he had no control over and would carry the rest of his life, often in great pain and suffering. "And I've had it since I was a child, so my case is more severe and doesn't respond well to treatment. That's why I'm here. The doctors in Mexico didn't think they could help me further, but Dr. Yonan convinced my father he could." Luca looked down at himself and then me again. "So far, so good. Asher might have been a horrible person, but Dr. Yonan's treatments are giving me relief for the first time in a long time."

I was happy to hear it and felt guilty now for what was to come. "There's an excellent chance this facility will shut down," I said. "I'm so sorry."

Luca's next shrug had an air of acceptance I'd not seen in people three times his age and maturity. Living with illness since childhood had that effect, I'd noticed. Young adults who'd survived like he had often aged mentally and emotionally beyond their years.

"I'll deal with it," he said. "You want to ask me if I killed Asher."

Um. Okay then.

CHAPTER SEVENTEEN

That was a rapid change of topic I hadn't been prepared for. "Both of you," I said, nodding to Nora who had settled somewhat. "I assume the bruise and split lip weren't an accident."

She didn't respond, looking down at Luca's hands holding hers.

"It's okay," he whispered to her. "You can trust her."

Nora peeked up then and met my eyes at last. "Ms. Pringle," she said in a crackling voice that would be lovely if she spoke up and without so much emotion, "Asher Wyatt was a horrible person." She burst into tears, Luca cradling her against him, rocking her a little.

"He hit her," Luca said then, fury flashing in his

dark eyes, jaw clenching though his hands never tightened, arms soft around her. "And no one did anything about it." He sagged. "Not even me."

"That wasn't your fault," Nora insisted.

"My father's right," Luca told her. "I am weak, or I would have protected you."

One hand rose and cupped his cheek and she smiled for the first time, weak and trembling, but a smile, nonetheless. "You're the strongest and bravest person I know."

As adorable and supportive as their moment was? Didn't soften my own anger enough to get past the truth. Turning a blind eye to bullying was one thing, but outright abuse? "Did you tell Dr. Yonan, Nora?"

She shook her head, sniffling and accepting the tissue Luca leaned forward to pluck from the yellow box on the coffee table. She blew her nose delicately then sighed and sat back, more relaxed and no longer vibrating with pent-up emotion. Though, when she spoke, the dead tone of her voice echoed with deeply embedded trauma and disassociation I knew would plague her for her lifetime if she didn't get help. "I couldn't," she said. "Asher…" she looked up at Luca again, who nodded and smiled a small, comforting smile. "Asher had something he was holding over me."

I assumed as much. And meant I had to make a leap of trust if I was going to get her to tell me anything. Knowing Boone wasn't going to be happy with the turn of events but certain this was the only way I'd get any answers, I reached out to Nora and patted her knee.

"I'm a registered therapist," I said. "Do you need my services?" She seemed confused while Luca beamed a smile at me.

"Anything you tell her is between you and her," Luca said. "Nora, you can talk to her because no matter what you say, she can't tell the cops."

This was a terrible idea if Nora's reaction was any indication. She perked immediately, crying again and grasping my hand with hers, the tissue discarded, and her fear forgotten.

"I can't afford to hire you," she said.

Huh. What was she doing on the first floor if she wasn't wealthy? Then again, it was possible she was in one of the upstairs rooms and was only on this floor because of Asher and Luca. "Pro bono," I said. "My services are free. I'm here for you, Nora. Tell me what happened so I can help." And honestly? If she did kill Asher, I'd be on the stand defending her attack as self-defense at this point and anyone who argued it would have to look at photos of her bruise and broken lip and tell me she wasn't trying to keep herself safe.

But that wasn't what Nora had to share. "Asher and I have known each other for a long time," she said. "His car accident? The one that put him here?" I hadn't known he was in an accident, but that answered a question I hadn't asked yet, so I let her carry on with a nod of encouragement. "He told the police I was driving. And I let him."

"You weren't, though, were you?" She shook her head when I finished that statement for her. "Why did you lie for him?"

She looked at Luca one more time then faced me with determination on her pale face. "I used to sell drugs to Asher and his friends," she said. "It's how I paid for school. I told everyone I got a scholarship, but that wasn't true. My father was part of a gang and when he died, I took over selling for his bosses."

Not the best news. "Asher threatened to tell the authorities," I said.

"He already had two DUIs," she said, "and he was going to have to go to prison if he got caught again. So, he forced me to lie and tell the police I had the accident, and he was the passenger." She seemed to strengthen as she went on, like telling her story gave her more than relief, but courage and a measure of renewal. The desperately pale color in her cheeks warmed to a light pink, the dark circles not so pronounced, and her lovely voice smoothed out while she finished. "I haven't sold in two years," she said. "I got out, made a deal with the gang. But Asher still threatens me every chance he gets. And while he lived, I had to do what he said."

I didn't want to know what he'd forced her to do, though I took my job as her therapist seriously and meant what I'd offered. So, as long as she'd have me, I'd be here for her and would likely learn every horrid detail, even if it was from her prison cell. For now, I let the minutia fall to the wayside.

"What happened to Asher, Nora?" That was the weighty question hanging over the three of us, but to my surprise, both Luca and Nora exchanged startled looks and shook their heads in unison.

"We don't know," Luca answered for them both. "I swear, Ms. Pringle. Neither one of us hurt him or saw what happened."

"I know you saw me in the back hallway earlier, Nora," I said.

She nodded. "I didn't know what to do so I left," she told me. "I just wanted someone to help." She started crying again, softly this time, not so hopeless, Luca's arm around her seeming to give her further courage. "You know what? Given the chance, I might have done something to fight back. But I didn't. I was here with Luca. He's the only one who understands."

He cradled her against his chest, cheek on the top of her hair, face grim. "I know you know who my father is." I let out a little breath and waved at him to go on. "So, yes, I do understand. But I'm not my father, Ms. Pringle. Being ill has taught me to respect life, not to discard it like he does. And as horrible a person as Asher was, I would have much rathered he get what was coming to him legally and socially than in death."

Maybe Boone wouldn't believe them, or Cherise, but I did. At least, until I learned otherwise. "Thank you for your candor," I said. "Do either of you have any idea who could have done this?"

They exchanged another look, while Nora sadly faced me and squeezed my hand this time. "Thalia," she whispered. "I'm sorry, she hated him. And she was so volatile all the time. He tormented her mercilessly. I heard her threaten to hurt and kill him multiple times before today."

That didn't bode well. "Anyone else?"

"Look into Jose Delgato," Luca said. "There was some kind of deal going on between them, but I have no idea what." He was on my list for sure.

"It's probably nothing," Nora said then, almost stopping herself until Luca encouraged her. "I don't know if it has anything to do with Asher, but there's something off about that intern, Gray Fender." I'd been thinking the same thing despite his earlier kindness to Thalia. Sneaking around didn't encourage trust by any means. And yes, I'd been sneaking, too, but I was paid to do that, thanks. Which had me thinking about why he would be and if he was more than just an intern. "He gives me the creeps. He's always asking questions, poking his nose into stuff."

Luca was frowning, nodding. "He's off for sure," he said. And, as an intern, would also have access to drugs.

"Thank you," I said, rising. "I'll leave you both to rest. I know Detective Boone is going to have questions, but like I said, Nora, you're my client now, so anything you want kept between us is between us. I'll be here when he talks to you, all right?"

She seemed relieved, even rose to hug me quickly before flushing and backing off. "Thank you, Ms. Pringle," she said. "It means a lot." I wondered how many people she'd had in her life she could trust and was confident she'd make a full recovery because anyone who could still believe in another person after what she'd been through?

Was stronger than she knew.

CHAPTER EIGHTEEN

I wasn't expecting to find none other than Gray Fender standing outside Luca's door, leaning against the wall with a grin on his face and a little nod for me. That attitude made me pause to see what he had to say, especially in light of what Luca and Nora had just said.

If Gray had been eavesdropping and knew they told me to be wary of him he didn't show it, his hazel eyes on level with mine behind his glasses, lean body leaning in with his hands tucked in his pockets, all casual and cocky and really irritating me in my present state of mind.

"I thought you might like to know a thing or two I've picked up," he said. "You know, for the case." I nodded and did my best to show interest without judgment while he squirreled closer, almost vibrating, nose twitching and a rather unhealthy light in his eyes. "Those two?" He tipped his chin toward Luca's closed door. "Been thick as all get out since she and Asher arrived. It was why young Master Wyatt bullied Luca, I think. Asher didn't want to give up his ownership of Nora and she was getting a bit of a backbone at first thanks to Luca. That died pretty quick." He winked like the pun was intended. "Asher hated Luca and the feeling was mutual."

"What did Asher have against Thalia?" I was more interested in that than what I'd already uncovered on the other side of the door.

Gray shrugged, though his delight at dishing hadn't faded. "The guy hated everyone. Including his parents and himself. So, maybe he didn't need a reason." I actually bought that. "Besides, he was the richest kid on the block until she showed up. He hated that kind of competition. Needed to be the boss of her and everyone." He glanced over my shoulder as though to be sure we weren't being observed. "I take it you were aware he had Yonan under his thumb?" I didn't acknowledge it because something about Gray's tea spilling sat wrong with me. He didn't seem to notice, carrying on as though he'd been aching to tell someone everything he knew and wasn't he just so clever for digging up dirt on everyone? "Funny how Asher ended up in here," he said, "for court-mandated addiction counseling, along with that girlfriend of his." He meant Nora. "A normal person would be in prison." Well, no argument there. Money bought more than it solved in some cases. Might not be fair, but it was how the world worked. "I hear Asher wasn't just being treated for addiction, though. Rumor has it he had some serious nerve damage in his neck and back from the accident." That triggered a thought if it was true. Boone and I both wondered why Asher hadn't reacted to being dosed. What if he didn't know? Could it be the damage left him without feeling in the area he was jabbed? I filed that bit away and let Gray ramble on. "I wouldn't be surprised if Asher died from his own stupidity, high on something, and fell down the stairs on his own trying to torture Ms. Vesterville."

That was uncomfortably close to what I'd suggested to the detective, minus the dosing. "You seem to know an awful lot about an awful lot," I said. "Might I ask what you were doing listening in to Dr. Yonan's private conversation with Faith Yale in his office earlier tonight?"

Gray's face transformed in a flash from wicked delight to sullen closure, backing away a bit, eyes squinting as he reined himself in. "Good luck with the investigation," he said before hurrying off. Huh, that was an about-face. Why would he share all that he knew and then get defensive over being caught doing what he seemed to do best? There was more to Gray Fender than met the eye, for certain, and it was time to find out what he was really up to. But that meant help, and that meant Boone.

I paused on my way back down the hall in search of the detective, lingering at Faith's door a moment before knocking on impulse. She called out and I entered, the light on, the young woman clearly unable to sleep, propped up in bed with a book in her lap.

"Ms. Pringle," she said in her breathy voice. "Come in, please." She set the book aside, patting the edge of her bed and I joined her, surprised at her openness. "I'm so sorry about everything. How is Thalia?"

Her concern touched me more than she knew. "She's resting," I said. "Thank you for being kind to her, Faith. She hasn't had it easy."

Faith nodded, patting my hand. "I totally understand," she said. "In case you missed it, all of us on this floor come from families with far too much money and not nearly enough compassion or sense." She laughed, but it was bitter and brittle. "Sorry," she said then. "I know I shouldn't complain. I have so much more than most."

"But not what you really want." I squeezed her hand, letting my inner therapist out and wishing I'd brought Belladonna with me. She had a knack for getting people to open up even I sometimes lacked.

Faith didn't seem to need encouragement, however, and I immediately recognized her willingness to talk as a deep craving for attention she obviously never got from her family. "No," she agreed. "Poor little rich girl." She coughed delicately into one hand, so frail I worried for her. "I'm fine, really. This is what happens when you think beauty comes from zero percent body fat and social media filters." She sagged back into her pillows. "They call it an eating disorder. I call it my own little hell."

Anorexia nervosa explained a lot about her appearance and her delicate state. Years spent abusing her body with lack of nutrition would leave her with that thin hair and dry skin, the almost skeletal appearance of her. A giant wash of compassion for her and her history had me shaking off the investigation in favor of her mental health.

"If there's anything I can do," I said, "I'm happy to help, Faith."

She smiled at that. "So kind, thank you. But I have what I need here." She exhaled slowly, happily. "Amir, I mean, Dr. Yonan, he's such a treasure." She perked when she talked about him, the sheer force of her happiness disturbing. "He's been so kind, and his treatments are working. I'm feeling more the me I always wanted to be for the first time ever." She laughed at that. "Did that even make sense?"

I nodded. Several things were making sense, actually, only I hoped I was wrong about one of them. "You're very close," I said, tippytoeing around the accusation because if what I was thinking was true, this was one more reason for Yonan to lose his license.

She sighed dreamily and nodded. "I can honestly say I wouldn't be here if it wasn't for him. He's my hero."

And while it might have just been unnatural attachment due to her neglect and broken ideas of what love was, I had a terrible feeling her affection wasn't one-sided. From what I'd seen, I didn't have conclusive proof by any means. However, I knew very well therapists made the terrible mistake of falling for their patients, so such a thing wasn't a huge stretch, was it? A sick feeling stirred in my stomach for the young woman before me, anger aimed at the older, should be wiser and certainly professional doctor who may or may not be taking advantage.

Conclusion jumping aside, all of the above led me to a very uncomfortable line of questions I had to ask Dr. Amir Yonan. Because if Asher Wyatt was blackmailing Nora, who was to say he didn't find out unhappy truths about Faith that he'd then used against the doctor?

Motive for murder, anyone?

CHAPTER NINETEEN

I left Faith with more questions than answers and decided to focus on Thalia. Dr. Yonan's downfall could wait, though I'd be making sure the young woman who'd fallen under his rather unhealthy influence was safe from him, too.

Momma Bear wasn't retreating even an iota and seemed to have expanded her protective reach exponentially.

My attempts thereafter to track down and talk to Jose turned up nothing. Wherever he'd gone, I had to assume Boone was in the know. When the detective texted me, I joined him in the quiet café adjacent to the dining hall, the tall, handsome cop already brewing coffee behind the counter when I arrived. He seemed more than capable with the complicated machine and grinned when I leaned against the counter with a weary smile.

"Latte, right?" Hissing steam foamed a small container of milk he then hovered over a steaming cup of coffee, the aroma so delicious I almost went over the counter to grab it from him.

"Yes, please," I said, surprised at my demure tone because this was no time for flirting. "I take it a stint as a barista is on your resume somewhere?" He handed over the mug, a playful leaf decorating the surface. I sipped and sighed in delight while he chugged out a double shot of espresso for himself before circling to sit at one of the tables. I joined him, Boone's notebook appearing as he answered after a long drink of heady caffeine.

"Two years in college," he said. "Most fun I ever had at a job."

"You missed your calling, then," I said, cupping the mug in both hands, my tired body cold and needing the warmth more than I thought. "Might want to throw over the whole death business and open a coffee shop in a cute little seaside town."

He winked. "Know of any cute little seaside towns where I might be welcome?"

Yeah, okay, a little flirting never hurt anyone, especially after everything I'd been through. "I'm sure I can think of one."

His chuckle had a lovely ring to it. "Until then, shall we compare notes?"

I hesitated, only because I didn't want to shatter this lovely camaraderie we shared or the illusion of connection. Boone groaned a little as I paused, shaking his head, but without any malice.

"Just tell me what you did," he said. "I'll forgive you."

"What makes you think I need or want your forgiveness?" I arched an eyebrow and then sighed. And told him everything I was able to after informing him of exactly what I'd done for Nora.

His reaction wasn't what I was expecting, however. "It sounds like Ms. Teres has never had anyone take her side before." Boone stared down at his notebook, his own mug between his hands, resting on the table in quiet repose. "I understand, and while it's not making my job any easier, Seph, I applaud your compassion." He looked up then, those eyes I was learning to adore almost haunted. "Is that a thing for you? Taking on those who need to be fixed? Adopting the broken?" His soft laugh had a hitch to it.

"Not usually," I said. "I try to keep things professional. I prefer my personal life to be calm and peaceful." That had me wincing. "Though maybe fate doesn't agree with me on that desire."

Boone sat back, crossing one ankle over his other knee, toying with his pen in his right hand, left arm draping over the back of his chair as he watched me with a careful expression. His belt-buckle B winked at me in the dim light. But rather than carry on the conversation we'd been having, he started a new one.

"I looked into Asher Wyatt's car accident," he said, "and his record. Turns out the whole mess was quashed. I know the judge who signed off on Asher's treatment." His face contorted with a flare of resentment. "Let's just say I'm not surprised Asher was here and not in jail."

"And the only reason Nora is," I said, "is to keep her in line."

He nodded in agreement. "Looks that way. She's lucky. He could have just thrown her under the bus."

"Except if he did that, she'd be free to tell the authorities he was driving." Nora's story checked out to me.

"There was one gossip magazine that tried to out Asher," Boone said, leaning in to check his notes. "They're in the process of being sued by the family. *Truth or Bare*. Ever heard of it?"

I shook my head. "I can ask the girls. Anything from Jose or Dr. Yonan?"

"I'm working on it," he said. "Still waiting on word from a few friends in other departments. I'll fill you in when I know more."

Why did I get the impression he was stonewalling me? I leaned toward him with a wry smile and enough disbelief written on my face he laughed.

"I promise," he said, raising his right hand to join the oath.

"Uh-huh," I said. "You cops are all the same. Promises, promises."

His smile faded somewhat. "You dated a cop?" Why did he make that leap?

"Married and divorced an FBI agent," I said.

Boone's grin returned. "There's your problem," he said.

That made me laugh. "The last thing I expected from you was that same old macho bravado,

Boone."

He shrugged, looking up at me through thick, dark lashes, sexy smile returned. "I'm full of surprises, Seph."

I just bet he was. And despite everything? I was actually interested in finding out what kind of surprises, because *yum*. Just. *Yum*.

"What are you doing?" I spun, amusement and flirty attitude gone, to find Calliope standing at the entry to the café, glaring at both of us.

"Working the case, sweetie," I said. "Are you okay?"

"That's not what it looked like to me," she snarled, arms crossing over her chest. "If you don't mind, detective, my girlfriend's safety and wellbeing are a bit more important than you hitting on my mom."

Okay, that was uncalled for and highly inappropriate (even if it was true, but nope). "Young lady," I said.

"Ms. Garett," Boone interrupted me, standing and finishing his espresso with a single swallow. "Ms. Pringle." He exited past my daughter who watched him go with visible fury, face tight and body trembling before she turned back to scowl at me, cheeks bright pink in her anger.

"What is wrong with you?" She stormed off before I could say a word or shut her down, the echo of her question only adding to my weariness. I took a moment to gather myself, to stare into the dregs of the coffee Boone made me, alternating between anger at my kid, guilt for taking even a moment to remind myself I was a woman who still had years left to her, and resignation I was a terrible person who needed to get her priorities straight.

Just a bit of a complicated process, but I managed. And, when I finally did, I went looking for my kid because we needed to talk. I knew very well her reaction wasn't about Boone or me, but her worry about Thalia. Still, though I hadn't yet started dating officially, Calliope's hurt when I'd divorced her father still lingered. And yet, I couldn't bring myself to believe she'd begrudge me happiness when the time came, right?

The whole time factor was the crux of it, though. I had to put the girls first.

After this was over? We'd see. But it was nice, too, to know I was actually ready to get out there again, to maybe find someone who fit me for me, who I could see myself spending time with, if not the rest of my life.

Callie hadn't made it far, sitting at one of the tables in the corner of the dark dining hall, the sound of her weeping drawing me to her. I sat next to her and waited for her to come to me, a lesson I'd learned the hard way. No more supportive mom who didn't respect her boundaries. I didn't move, didn't speak, just let her have her moment. And when she finally did decide to hug me, it was in a rush of motion and crying, her arms tight around my neck, while I rocked her a little and whispered her name over and over.

"It's going to be okay," I said. "No matter what, honey. It's going to be okay."

"How do you know that?" She leaned back, lost in her grief and despair, my beautiful and sweet and emotional and brilliant daughter's resilience challenged to the limit.

"Because you're here," I said, stroking her bangs back from her forehead, "and Thalia is here, and I'm with you. We're all safe and together for now. The rest will sort itself out."

Callie's lips vibrated as more tears fell. "I'm scared, Mom." She reached into her pocket and held her hand out. I looked down and caught my breath as the empty syringe rolled forward in her palm. "I think Thalia killed Asher and I don't know what to do about it."

CHAPTER TWENTY

"Where did you find this?" I reached for a napkin and wrapped the syringe in it, setting it aside. The fact my daughter's prints would now be on it wasn't lost on me.

"Thalia's trash can." Calliope choked on the words, her hands clasping together so tightly her knuckles whitened. "I overheard Gray talking to one of the uniforms. He said Asher was drugged, that it might have been what killed him." The intern again. He was as nosy as me, it seemed. But what motive drove him? "Mom, what was this doing in Thalia's garbage? Do you think it means..." she broke off with a choking inhale.

Considering used needles and syringes were meant to be disposed of in a sharps box—and I knew for a fact there was one in Thalia's room—the appearance of the item in her trash had me concerned. "Maybe Jose put it there by accident." I didn't think much of the nurse, so such a slip in protocol wasn't a huge mental stretch.

"*Is* that how Asher died?" I hesitated to answer because I didn't know the truth yet. "*Did* he OD or something?"

"No," I finally said. Sighed. "Not self-inflicted, at least. But he was sedated, we think. Or drugged with something. And." I squeezed her hands. "Callie, Boone and I already looked at the video footage. There's no way Thalia was the one who injected Asher. The timing doesn't fit." Which had my mind turning.

"Then what was it doing in her room?" Calliope seemed willing to accept hope, her anxiety fading somewhat.

"It could be nothing, sweetie," I said, standing and retrieving the syringe. "It's probably a coincidence and fault of the nurse, like I said." Saying it out loud seemed to comfort her even while my own mind called me a liar. Though the possibility loomed that the person who had injected Asher decided to find a way to shift the blame to someone already under scrutiny rather than the worry Thalia herself might have deposited it there. Because she made an excellent target, right? "Let me take care of this. Your job is Thalia."

Callie nodded, misery still on the surface. The sight of it caught my breath as I realized what I'd said. Because whose job was it to take care of

Calliope? Mine.

I hugged her tight. "I love you so much," I said, choking up myself as she embraced me back, no holds barred, both of us swaying together. "You are so strong and brave and amazing that I forget sometimes you need support just as much as Thalia." Callie tried to shake her head, but I went on anyway. "You don't have to take this on alone. You're not alone, my sweet girl. I'm here and I'm not going anywhere."

Calliope cried again, this time ugly and broken, the kind of weeping that came from months of pent-up hurt and worry and fear. It took her a good ten minutes to empty her reservoir of agony and I let her, not speaking, just holding her and rocking with her and doing my best to give her the space and safety to relieve herself of everything that weighed her down.

By the time she was done, and I'd handed her a fresh napkin from the table to clean herself up, she seemed calm and composed.

"Thanks, Mom." Calliope looked up through her wet lashes, hazel eyes soft and warm. "I know I fight you sometimes." She snorted. "A lot. You raised me to stand up for myself and I turn that against you. I'm sorry." I tried to speak but she wasn't done. "I don't say it enough, but I love you, too. So much, Mom. And I'm so grateful for you. I wouldn't be who I am without you. Thank you for letting me be who I am and never letting me fall."

Now I was ugly crying, her turn to hug me and hold me a moment while I choked on the release of my guilt and worry about her. Mine didn't take ten minutes, though a solid thirty seconds went by before I took the last clean napkin from the table's place setting and demolished it with the results of my emotional outburst.

I smiled at my kid, and she smiled back, tremulous and small, but present in her eyes, so I knew we were both okay. Just tired, and ready for this to be done.

Which meant I needed to get back to it. "Let's go talk to Thalia," I said, holding out my hand. "Together."

Calliope exhaled long and soft then nodded. "I'm ready for the truth, Mom."

So was I.

Jose was exiting Thalia's room, head down and refusing to meet my eyes when I passed him. I almost backtracked and left Calliope to sit with Thalia, but I needed to talk with the Vesterville heiress and Jose wasn't going anywhere.

I found Thalia awake and patting Belladonna, but they weren't alone. Gray Fender excused himself the moment Callie and I arrived, scooting out past me while Thalia ignored us, her focus on the lovely white cat in her lap, soothing hum matching the feline's purr.

"What did he want?" Calliope hurried to her girlfriend and checked her over, while I stared at the now-closed door and wondered the same thing. He was an intern, so it was possible he was just checking in. Still, his rapid exit and lack of any equipment or apparently scheduled procedure had me as curious as I was concerned.

"Nothing," Thalia said in a small, soft voice. "Everything is fine." She looked up, blinking and smiling in such a vague way I instantly suspected trouble.

"Thalia, did he give you something?" I stopped at her left side, Callie on her right, looked in her eyes closely, touched her cheek. The faint flush there and the widening of her pupils had me furious all over again. She'd been drugged.

"Not him," she blinked at me. "Jose always does it."

No wonder he wouldn't meet my gaze on the way past me. Were these Dr. Yonan's continuing orders? Didn't matter. I was at the absolute end. "I'll be back," I snarled at Callie. "And if I'm arrested for murder, it's justified."

My daughter's chin rose. "Go kick his ass, Mom."

The fact she just asked me to fight her battle for her? Made me far happier than it should have. I didn't get to go hunting, however, the soft buzz of my phone bringing me up short with my fingers on the door handle. I thumbed the message open, Boone's text giving me more pause.

Hubbs said Asher OD'd, some kind of drug that affected his heart. He confirmed Wyatt's nerve damage, possible he never even felt the injection, might have felt pressure but nothing more.

I struggled to care at the moment. *Jose just dosed Thalia against my permission*, I sent back, anger in every letter. *I'm going to confront him.* Oh, how I hoped he was the murderer. Please, let it be him. He'd suffer and I'd see to it.

Wait for me, Boone sent back.

Yeah. Whatever. I had a head of steam on, and Calliope wasn't the only one at the end of her rope. I stormed out of the room and stalked my way down the hall to the lobby, looking for Jose and not seeing him. The offices corridor lured me forward, hunt for the employee lounge or somewhere the hulking nurse could be hiding keeping my momentum up. But when I ended up at the reception desk outside Dr. Yonan's office, the sight of Gray Fender picking the lock of that same doorway? Had me taking out my aggression on him instead.

"You have a lot of explaining to do," I snarled.

Gray spun with a squeak, tucking his hands behind his back like I hadn't just caught him in the middle of a B&E during a murder investigation. "It's not what it looks like," he said, far too cocky for my liking.

"It looks like you're interfering in a police matter," I said, knowing I sounded testy and unable to rein in my attitude. "That makes you look guilty of something, Gray. Maybe murder."

He shook his head, pocketing the tools he'd been using, shrugging and grinning at me. "To the contrary," he said. "I'm looking for evidence, not trying to hide it."

What? "What are you talking about?"

"I haven't been entirely honest," he said, sticking out one hand. "Gray Mitchell, editor and publisher of *Truth or Bare*, and do I have a story for you."

Oh, crap.

CHAPTER TWENTY-ONE

I barely got to acknowledge what he'd just said when he dodged past me after I didn't immediately accept his hand.

"At least," he said, "I *will* have a story for you and the detective, but I still have some digging to do."

"If you print anything about Thalia," I said, shocked at the ominous sound of my threat, but meaning every word.

Gray just laughed as he hurried away. "I've been sued before. Ciao!" And he was gone, leaving me livid, shaking and wanting to scream at someone, anyone. Because while it was now clear to me the so-called intern and admitted journalist wasn't the murderer, Thalia's whole life was not just under threat due to her health and looming possibility of arrest, she now had to worry about the court of public opinion. I had zero doubts someone like Gray Fender/Mitchell would take great delight in publishing horrible things about her just for ratings and magazine sales.

We'd see about that.

My phone alerted me to a text I could barely read through my anger.

Where are you? Boone had to be worried and with very good reason.

Offices, I sent back, already striding back down the hall, my hunt for Jose interrupted but not halted. *Gray Fender's real name is Mitchell. He runs* Truth or Bare.

Gotcha, Boone sent back. *You didn't wait for me. Don't do anything drastic.*

Again with the whatever, because he didn't know drastic.

I looked up from my phone as I took a side corridor, still looking for the staff room, and finally spotted Jose ahead. The sight of Faith in her wheelchair beside him, the tall nurse bent over her, handing her something, had my blood boiling over. But before I could interrupt, Jose looked up, spotted me, and hurried off, Faith tucking her hands and whatever he'd given her into her lap, pinched and nervous expression making me stop to confront her.

"What's going on, Faith?" I caught the tears on her cheeks, had to pull myself back from the raging demand in my mind to take Jose apart and put on my therapy hat if only to keep from terrifying the poor young woman with the level of my rage at the moment.

She didn't seem afraid of me per se, but something had triggered her hurt. Unlike our last conversation, she finally found the means to hold herself back. "I can't," she choked. "It will ruin him."

Who, Jose? Why did she care? And then it dawned on me through my anger even as heavy footsteps behind me stopped at my side and the now-familiar scent of Detective Boone tugged at my attention.

"Ms. Yale," he said, "I have some questions for you."

I glanced up at him, surprised, even more so when Dr. Yonan, trailing Boone, his arrival lost to me until then, pushed past the detective and placed himself between Boone and Faith.

"Don't say anything," he told her. "Despite the fact she's done nothing wrong," the doctor said to us then, face lined and weary and full of anxiety, golden skin tone now yellow and aged, shoulders stooped, his tie missing and shirt badly rumpled. All his dark waves stuck out at odd angles, deep lines tugging his mouth down, visible despite his beard. "She wants a lawyer. Leave her alone."

That protectiveness told me the feelings Faith expressed in so many words were returned after all. That was unfortunate. I hadn't wanted to be right despite knowing I was.

"Dr. Yonan," I said, now level despite my continuing disgust at how he handled this facility, "you do know how unethical it is to carry on a relationship with a patient when she's in your care?"

He flinched, Faith's crying louder now. Boone glanced at me with raised eyebrows while I went on. "You've just ruined any chance you have of retaining your license to practice."

He didn't get to deny it.

"It's all my fault," Faith wailed then, one hand reaching up to take his, the doctor turning to kneel next to her and attempt to soothe her. "I'm sorry, Amir. I love you and I ruined everything."

"It's all right, my dear," he said. "It's going to be all right."

I'd said the same thing to Calliope. In this case, it really wasn't, so was I lying to my daughter, too? At least I wasn't almost three times the age of a vulnerable young woman who was in my care, right? Yes, I was judging him, though when he looked up, the strain in his face, the grief in his eyes, had me sighing.

"I know what it looks like," he said, gruff and with a hitch in his voice. "Believe me, I know. Neither of us planned on this." He met her eyes while she gently touched his cheek with shaking fingertips. "I assure you we've been nothing but discreet."

I glanced at Boone who didn't show what he was thinking or feeling past the steady and level stare he fixed the both of them with while I fought the need to toss my hands and turn my back on the whole sordid situation.

"You've refused to tell me where you were at Asher Wyatt's time of death," Boone said. "Is it because you were together?" Oh, that was a problem.

Yonan shook his head, however, while Faith watched. "I simply wanted my lawyer, detective," the doctor said. "But if you must know, I was in my office." He glanced at the young woman next to him with a guilty expression. Why, because he didn't alibi her? She squeezed his hand, looking up to meet the detective's eyes.

"And I was in my room," she said. "Despite what you think, we haven't done anything wrong." She turned to me then. "Our love is real, but we've been chaste."

There was that much, at least.

Boone pulled out his notebook and pen and jotted a quick line.

"Thank you for finally answering my question," he said without a trace of sarcasm. "I'm going to ask you another now and I hope you're done lying to me."

Dr. Yonan didn't respond, but he also didn't seem as rebellious as before, so maybe the truth coming out had ended his reticence. Since he was ruined now regardless.

"Did Asher Wyatt know about both of you?" I had the same question in my mind now that I had confirmation of what I'd suspected all along and was rewarded with a stiff nod from Dr. Yonan.

"He threatened to expose us," Yonan admitted.

"Jose knows too," I said, the flash of insight making the doctor sigh.

"Yes," he said.

"Jose was working for Asher," Faith blurted then, Yonan softly trying to hush her, but the young woman refused to listen. Maybe he was willing to share now, but he clearly wanted her to stay out of it. Faith wasn't having that. "He was digging up dirt on everyone." Sounded a lot like a particular intern/shock journalist I'd just had a run-in with. Was Gray working with Asher too? Paying him for information?

"Faith, what did Jose just give you?" I pointed at her lap as her hands twitched in protectiveness over the item he'd handed off.

"Footage," she whispered. "I don't know how he got it, but Asher claimed he had video of Amir and me." She flushed, shook her head while the doctor gaped at her. "You didn't know, but I was paying him for it, Amir. I just wanted to protect you." She handed him the small, black jump drive that she'd hidden in her lap. A drive the detective immediately held his hand out for. Dr. Yonan reluctantly gave it to Boone while Faith wiped at her tears. "It should have been all over. Asher's dead and Jose took the money. He said this was the only copy."

And if she believed that I had a bridge to sell her. More than likely, Jose would have continued to blackmail her for years, but that wasn't my problem right now.

"Why was Asher so interested in dirt on everyone?" I had my guesses since he clearly didn't need money.

Faith's shrug was thin and defeated, expression now sullenly resentful. "No reason," she said. "He was just a hateful piece of trash who liked to ruin people."

I wasn't going to argue with her there.

"I'm so sorry, Amir," Faith said while he patted her hand, putting a bit of distance between them that made her frown.

"It doesn't matter now," he told her absently, still focused on me and the detective. "As you can both see, neither of us is guilty of anything to do with Asher Wyatt."

The state board could deal with him, I was done. "I'm more concerned about your lack of ability to follow my direct orders," I said, my anger still simmering.

"I have no idea what you mean," he shot back, surging to his feet.

"Jose gave Thalia medication against my strict request," I said, shaking now as the hit of adrenaline I'd put on hold for this little conversation resurfaced. "Explain yourself."

"I assure you," he said then, voice low and vibrating, "my care of Thalia Vesterville has been nothing but with her best interests at heart. I ordered nothing of the sort and have followed your instructions—as misguided as they are—to the letter since your arrival. Now, if you'll excuse us, I have calls to make."

The doctor wheeled Faith away, neither of them going anywhere, not really, so I let them go, scowling now. Except the young woman turned to speak as he pushed her away.

"Jose was angry with Asher, Ms. Pringle," she said. "I don't know why, but they were fighting over something that had Jose very upset."

Interesting. I was more concerned about the Vesterville heiress and her condition, however, and Jose's act of medicating her. "Thalia." I blurted her name, Boone's expression now concerned.

"Right behind you," he said.

Panic gripped me as I spun and headed for the girls, Boone following me without a word. If Jose acted on his own? Had he been trying to do the same thing to her as he possibly did to Asher? Was Thalia's life in danger, too?

Jose had a lot of questions to answer.

CHAPTER TWENTY-TWO

To my relief (my poor heart really couldn't take much more, I swear), Thalia was quietly talking with Calliope when the detective and I arrived, Belladonna's meowing welcome crashing my adrenaline spike and forcing me to lean against the bed a moment, so I didn't fall down.

"Mom, are you okay?" Callie rose to hug me, but I forced a smile because she didn't need me falling apart on her right now.

"Just checking in," I said. "You two are all right?"

Thalia seemed wonky still, but only vaguely so and I wondered about Jose. Gray had been in the room with her when I'd arrived, just before she showed signs of being drugged. Had he interrupted Jose? Perhaps the nurse hadn't had time to deliver a full dose. Whatever the truth, she appeared a bit out of it, but nothing like earlier, so I let out a long sigh of tension and backed off.

"Don't leave her," I whispered to my daughter as I exited the room with Boone, closing the door and leaning my back against it while I clenched my jaw against the need to cry.

"I'll post a uni," Boone said, one gentle hand on my arm making my tendency toward weeping worse, but I didn't pull away.

"Thanks." I wrapped myself in control and opened my eyes, his beautiful ones staring down at me, so close if he'd just tipped his head a bit more and I'd reached up on my tiptoes, our lips would have easily connected. Boone seemed to have the same realization, a flare of heat passing through his gaze, hand trailing up my arm before he backed away a firm step and nodded to me, clearing his throat.

"Let's talk," he said. I almost choked on that suggestion. "About the case."

Oh. Right. The case. Whoops.

There was a small nook at the far end of the corridor with a pair of chairs under tall windows. I couldn't believe it was still dark out. Surely this never-ending night would finally turn over into morning at some point? I sighed as I sank into the plush velvet wingback, sinking into the firm but embracing cushions while Boone did the same.

"Looks like Dr. Yonan and Faith both had motive, but no means," he said, deep voice lush and quiet. "Though it's possible they are lying and did the deed together if their safety was threatened."

I wasn't sure I'd put that kind of desperate act past Yonan at this point, but I had other suspects who seemed more likely. "One for the back burner for now," I said. "Next?"

"Gray Fender, sorry, Mitchell," Boone frowned as he fished out his notebook. "Good catch on that. I hadn't heard back on him yet."

"He admitted it to me when I caught him in a B&E attempt," I said. "But it sounds like he doesn't have motive. To the contrary. This is a giant boon for him." I winced. "Sorry, bad choice of word."

He shrugged. "I'm used to it. And I agree with you. I doubt Asher would have any means of blackmailing him Mitchell wouldn't turn against him with his own dirt. So, let's set him aside for the moment." The detective tapped the page in front of him with the tip of his pen. "Jose hasn't been forthcoming and now that we have Faith's evidence, I'll admit I'm leaning."

"Does that mean we can drop the Thalia thing?" Not likely, since I had evidence that I still hadn't handed over to Boone. I tried not to feel guilty about it, because for all I knew it was an innocent mistake and meant nothing. Time to clear that up. I fished the wrapped syringe out of my pocket and handed it over, his startled expression only lasting a moment.

"I have no idea if it means anything," I said, "but Callie found that in Thalia's trash. There's a good possibility, considering the footage we watched, the one who dosed Asher planted that in Thalia's room to shift blame. We should check the footage again and see if anyone entered." I already knew Jose had, and Gray. Narrowed my list considerably.

Boone didn't comment, the napkin reclosed and set aside for the moment as he went on as if I hadn't just given him reason to think Thalia magically found a way to inject Asher that we didn't know about.

"That leaves Nora Teres," Boone said, "and Luca Diaz."

I thought about it a long moment. "I really want to believe them," I said.

"But," the detective said.

"Luca didn't fight back when Asher bullied him," I said. "Maybe he didn't value his own safety enough. I got the impression from him his worst nightmare is to turn into his father." I hardly blamed him.

"But." Boone repeated the word with finality.

"Acting out to defend someone he loved?" I shrugged. "It's a real possibility. Asher died after hitting Nora. That may have been the trigger Luca needed to act. And it's more than likely she'd alibi him to make sure he got away with it."

"Agreed." Boone nodded over his notes. "You really are good at this, Seph."

Part of me wished I wasn't. I lifted my weary head from the back of the chair, feeling like it weighed a million pounds and wondering if anyone would notice if I had a little bitty nap right there. "We have to find Jose."

Boone stood, tucking away his notes and pen, but when I tried to rise, he shook his head with a gentle touch to my shoulder. "You're beat," he said. "Close your eyes for a few minutes. I'll track him down and come get you."

I wanted to argue, but I really was wiped out. "Don't you dare cut me out now," I said.

He grinned. "Same. I'll be right back." I watched him stride away, blinking as my eyes closed and I tried to do what he said, what my body wanted.

Except my mind kept churning, refusing me rest despite my weariness and I finally had to admit defeat. With a groan, I pulled myself up and exhaled heavily before heading for the girls. I could at the very least peek in and make sure they were okay. For the umpteenth time that would never, ever end.

I was passing the corridor to the back hallway when I spotted movement and turned to look. Jose Delgato was hurrying through the doorway, heading for the exit to the greenhouse and the back stairs. Fired up all over again, I followed, reaching for my phone as I did, sending off a fast text to Boone.

I should have waited for the detective, but Jose's whole furtive attitude had me worried he might try to make a run for it, so I stayed in pursuit, keeping back enough he didn't notice, though it was more his focus on his task than my expert sneaking skills that kept me safe from getting caught. I had to jog to the door when he disappeared through it and down the stairs, discovering he'd already exited the greenhouse when I arrived.

I shivered, missing my coat but not wanting him to get away and pursued, catching sight of him circling to the left as I peeked out the back door to the greenhouse, further around the building than I'd gone before. The chill November wind cut through my thin dress, though I was grateful for my tights and boots, and I hugged myself as I pursued my quarry all the way to the other end of the building, sending a second text to Boone to identify my location. No way was I facing Jose alone at this point.

My head was down over my phone as I came around the corner, which meant I ran right into the person in question, though he seemed as startled to see me as I was him. The fact he was leaning over a dumpster, and it was his waggling feet I stumbled into led to a rather comical moment of him grunting and shimmying himself backward until he landed beside me with a heavy thud in the dark of the building's shadow.

And it suddenly wasn't funny anymore.

CHAPTER TWENTY-THREE

It had been only a short time since I'd been pursued through a creepy maze by someone who wanted to do me harm, and even I had to admit I'd not come out of the situation on Halloween without a measure of PTSD to deal with. I'd been trying to, naturally, but with all the drama around Thalia and Calliope, I'd put off really digging into the experience and rooting out the memory.

Which meant, as Jose leaned toward me, fists at his sides and belligerent expression threatening harm—as did everything about him—my fight, flight or freeze response kicked in.

You know me well enough by now, I assume, to guess which one came roaring out.

I'd kept up my judo classes and had another

reason to hug my teacher, Raeann, who'd assured me—and been proven right—short people like me with our low center of gravity could use that stature to advantage with the right training. Which meant, as I ducked a moment before Jose swung, my body knew instinctively how to tuck and dodge under the bigger, heavier man's attack and deliver a side kick to his right knee.

He went down as my boot landed hard, his outcry echoing in the darkness. I watched him fall, backing off so he couldn't lunge out and reach me, though that didn't seem to be on his agenda now that he'd hit the ground.

"That hurt!" I hadn't expected him to whine about it since he'd been ready to punch me.

"Good," I shot back, still vibrating from adrenaline. "Want some more or are you going to behave yourself?" Bravado, Seph? How gauche.

Someone came huffing out of the darkness, skidding to a halt next to me, Boone's concern turning to surprise and then amusement, even as he shucked off his peacoat and draped it around my shivering person. The scent of him surrounded me in a wave and wasn't helping my shock reaction any. Or maybe it was, and I simply wasn't in a position to appreciate it. Regardless, I was grateful for the warmth while Boone firmly cuffed the big nurse after dragging him, still whimpering and complaining, to his feet.

"She hit me," he grumbled. "That's assault."

"You swung first," I shot back.

"Enough," Boone said, the first hit of temper I'd

seen from him shutting Jose's response down. "Let's go inside and have a chat, shall we, Mr. Delgato?"

It wasn't until we were seated at a table in the dining room, one of Boone's uniforms standing guard behind Jose, that I finally returned the detective's coat, missing the weight of it almost immediately but squaring my shoulders. It wasn't like I needed that kind of support and I think I'd proven that over and over again.

Did that mean it was wrong to enjoy it?

A question for another time as Boone began his interrogation. "You've been lying to me all this time, Mr. Delgato," he said, characteristic bland whimsy in play. "I don't like being lied to."

Jose grunted something, head down, jaw jumping, but he finally sighed and nodded. "I was helping Asher find dirt on other residents and staff," he said.

"We are aware," Boone told him. Jose looked up, surprise passing over his face before he settled into that sullen petulance again, heavy brows giving him a brutish and rebellious look. "In fact, we are in possession of one of your thumb drives with a certain resident and doctor featuring in the surveillance." He tapped his notebook with his pen. "You do know blackmail is illegal?"

Of course, Jose did. "It was all Asher," he said.

I almost snorted. "I'm sure," I said. "All his idea, was it?"

Jose turned his head, still staring everywhere but at us. "He offered me money." The universal currency of betrayal and deceit.

"How much was he paying you?" Boone's pen hovered over the page, waiting for the answer.

"That's the thing," Jose snarled then, looking up at last. "He said he would but he didn't. That jerk owed me thousands and refused to pay." He went silent then, looking back and forth between us as if realizing he'd said too much.

Which he had. "You've just admitted to conspiracy to blackmail and given me an excellent motive for Mr. Wyatt's murder, Mr. Delgato." Boone's tone hadn't changed but there was a new tension in him I hadn't sensed before. Maybe I was learning his ways or perhaps it was just my imagination, but I doubted the latter while suspecting the former.

"I didn't kill him," Jose grumbled.

"Did you drug him?" Boone pressed a bit harder, but Jose shook his head.

"I just wanted my money," the nurse complained to us. "How could he pay me if he was dead?"

That was pretty solid logic, I had to admit, and from what I'd seen of Jose, excellent motivation to keep Asher alive. Which triggered a new question from me without waiting for Boone. "What was so important you decided to dig around in a compost bin, Mr. Delgato?" I realized I was hugging myself and firmly dropped my arms, hands resting on my thighs.

He glared at me. "My knee still hurts."

"Poor baby," I snapped. "Answer the question."

Jose's gaze flickered to Boone. "My camera."

Ah, the source of the footage he'd given Faith.

"Why would it be in the dumpster?"

"Because," he snarled at me, returning his attention when Boone didn't interrupt, "it was set up in the greenhouse in one of those stupid plants on the stairs and must have gotten chucked by the cops after the techs were done."

That had Boone sitting forward while I frowned. There was no way the forensics team or Boone's officers would have thrown out evidence. So, what actually happened to the item in question? Boone was all over it. "You had a camera in there when Mr. Wyatt died?" Why hadn't Jose said so? Surely it would exonerate him from murder. While incriminating him for blackmail, but the first was a better charge to bear, wasn't it?

Jose let out a long, angry sigh. "The camera's gone," he said. "I can't find it."

"And the footage?" Boone's tone had dropped another notch.

"Embedded on the camera," Jose said. "It's a nanny cam. I have to download it directly from the unit to see what's on it. Without it…" his shoulders moved in a vague shrug.

We needed to find that camera.

The officer led Jose away, Boone sitting back to stare at his notebook while I leaned in.

"Would the techs have taken it?" It had to be somewhere.

Boone shook his head. "If they'd found anything like that, they would have told me."

"Surely, they wouldn't have thrown anything out at an active crime scene." The idea appalled me, and

Boone's expression matched my feeling exactly.

"I doubt it," he said, "but worse things..." He perked then, looking up. "David, I need a team to go through that dumpster."

The officer paused with Jose in hand and nodded before the two exited the room. Boone's eyes turned to mine as he spoke.

"The answer might be on that camera," he said. Paused. "Are you ready for that?"

I nodded immediately. "For better or worse, I am. We need to know the truth, Boone."

His lips parted as though he had further comment, but he shook his head instead and smiled that slow, sexy smile of his that had my gaze lingering on his mouth for far too long. When I looked up again and our eyes locked, Boone leaned in to match me, close enough I could feel the warmth of his breath on my own lips when he spoke again.

"Why does it seem like I've known you forever?" I blinked, nodding as I realized that was exactly how I was feeling. "Strange, and as inappropriate as it is..." Boone inhaled slowly, not backing down. "When this is over."

He stopped for so long I took over. "I'm not looking for anything."

"Neither was I." His green eyes felt bottomless and devouring. "In fact, this was the last thing I ever thought I wanted again. But now, I'm not sure. As much as I thought I was, I'm not the type to walk away from something without finding out what might be." His head tilted, lights catching the silver in his dark hair and the scruff on his face. I felt a little mesmerized, likely from being overtired and overstimulated—in more ways than one—but it wasn't unpleasant, and I had to admit my attraction to him felt as satisfying as it did natural. "Seph, when this is over, can I call you?"

I caught my breath, heart pounding, then nodded. Even as we stared at one another for a long, aching moment that felt like it lasted forever.

And not nearly long enough.

I know I would have kissed him given another second or two. I'm absolutely positive of that fact, actually. I'd never felt such magnetism, such chemistry, with another human being as I did with Kellan Boone, and I suddenly wanted to know what that meant.

Not meant to be, at least right then and there.

"Detective." The female uniform's interruption came at the perfect time, it seemed, because when I scooted back in surprise at myself, now embarrassed by my lack of composure, it was obvious kissing him wasn't the best option, was it?

Oh, Seph. Kissing him was the *only* option.

"Yes, Kelly?" Boone didn't react one way or the other, as natural and collected as ever, bless him, giving me a moment to gather myself. I needed lessons in how to be more like him if I was going to continue to be welcome in state cases.

Wait, was that something I really wanted?

"The techs are on their way back," she said, low hum of resentment in her voice not lost on me. Why, was she jealous? Of me professionally or personally? Didn't matter. The question only made me tired.

"Thank you," he said. "I'm heading out myself to supervise the process." She left after a moment, looking like she had more to say but not bothering. Which left me alone with Boone again.

He stood, donning his coat as I joined him. "Let me take care of this," he said. "Now that we know there's evidence that can prove this case one way or the other, it's a good time for you to go get some rest."

I almost argued but nodded instead. "I'll be with the girls," I said, heading for the door, whole body heavy and really needing to sit down again but not willing to show him how tired I actually was.

"Seph." His soft call had me turning. Boone hadn't moved from the table, watching me go with his hands in his coat pockets. "I find you remarkable." And without another word, he turned and strode for the other door, gone before I could formulate a response.

I thought about him all the way to Thalia's room, I admit it. It was almost as if knowing the detective was this close to possession of proof freed my mind from the endless spiral of maybes, possiblies and could bes that I'd been contemplating when it came to the suspects in the case. Not to mention my exhaustion and layered worry about Thalia and Calliope. By the time I reached the door to the suite, I had half-convinced myself a date with Kellan Boone might be the very thing I needed in my life.

Had me smiling at the possibilities. Because I thought he was remarkable, too.

That state of mind was the reason it took me a

full five seconds of staring as I froze in the doorway to process what I was seeing, but as soon as I snapped out of my moment of shock, my temporary reprieve from stress was shattered as the scene before me crashed into me like a freight train.

"Thalia!" I reached for her as she stood over Calliope, my daughter asleep on the bed, her girlfriend's upraised hand clutching a syringe with a shining needle. "No!"

CHAPTER TWENTY-FOUR

Calliope started awake at my shout, letting out her own cry of surprise and fear as Thalia wavered over her, the syringe still aloft. A heavy humming growl rose from the covers next to my daughter, Belladonna leaping out and swiping at Thalia with the cat's courage ending in a long hiss.

That seemed to catch Thalia's attention like nothing else. She staggered back, arm lowering a little, her thin face falling from the flat, empty expression she'd harbored to a crumpled edge of hysteria. I hurried to her, taking the syringe away, noting it matched the one Calliope had shared with me and that the sharps box next to the bed had been jimmied open, clearly the source of Thalia's weapon.

She leaned into me, staring into my eyes with her

own glazed but filling with tears. "If we go to sleep forever," she whispered, "nothing can hurt us ever again." And then she buried her face in my neck and sobbed while Calliope scrambled out of bed, clutching Belladonna to her, terror on her face.

It was the first time I saw her afraid of Thalia and it didn't bode well for either of them.

I sat Thalia down on the bed, holding her wrists, but she didn't fight me or seem inclined to attack again. "Is that what you did to Asher, sweetheart?" I thought I knew better, but was I wrong? Had she somehow gotten her hands on a full syringe? If that's what he'd been given. I didn't even know that much yet. Jose's lax attention to his job could easily have allowed Thalia to nick something from his tray, but wouldn't he have noticed?

The real question was, would he have cared? Or did he supply it to her to ensure his claim of innocence was real and pushed Thalia over the edge into madness and murder to gain revenge without dirtying his own hands?

Of course, my mind raged through scenario after option after terrible idea while Thalia pulled herself together to answer. I watched the confusion on her face from my question turn to denial, the flicker of who she really was surfacing as though from a dream.

"I didn't kill anyone," she said, voice more normal. "What's going on? What happened?" She turned to find Callie staring at her in that same horrified way she'd worn since my shout roused her. "What did I do?"

My daughter shook her head, cradling Belladonna whose tail continued to thrash in agitation. "It's not your fault," she said, words crackling as she choked on them.

Thalia's head whipped around, contorting as she leaned into me again. "What did I do to Callie?"

"Nothing," I told her. "You're not well, Thalia. We're going to get you out of here and get you help."

"You keep saying that," she wailed. "But I'm still here."

"We're looking for a piece of evidence," I said, trying to reassure her. "It will prove what happened to Asher when he died."

She shook her head, thin hair falling out of her messy bun, hands shaking inside my grip. "I don't remember anything," she sobbed those words in heaving breaths that I felt physically, aching in my chest with each one increasing. "Why can't I remember?"

I hugged her, rocking her as I had Calliope not so long ago, meeting my daughter's troubled gaze and made the choice to spill everything if only to bring them some little comfort. "There's a nanny cam out there with the proof we need," I said. "Jose was working with Asher to get blackmailable details on everyone. According to him, the camera was in the plants at the bottom of the stairs at the greenhouse, the ones that were smashed when Asher fell. He thinks it was tossed when the techs left. Detective Boone is looking for it."

Thalia looked up as I spoke, mute and rather empty. When I finished, she reached around me and into the drawer of her bedside table, sliding it open. Her fingers lifted out a small, black square she deposited in my hands.

"This one?"

Oh. My. What? "Where did you get this?"

She shrugged, sagging as though all life was leaving her, hands supporting her face with her elbows propped on her thighs. "I don't know," she said. "I think I remember finding it, but it's all so foggy." She sat up a little bit, but it was clear she was at the end of her resilience. "I found it in my pocket earlier and put it in there. Is that the one?"

There was only one way to find out. "Callie..." I hesitated, not sure if I should leave them alone.

But my daughter shook her head firmly, coming to sit next to Thalia and setting Belladonna on the bed beside her. "We'll be fine," she said in a firm voice her horror and fear gone, replaced by determination. "I'll stay awake."

Was it wrong I lingered one more moment before kissing them both? I should have just trusted Callie, but without knowing what was actually going on with Thalia, it was hard to leave them alone. Still, I had no doubt now that my daughter had forewarning of danger, the time it took me to get this camera to Boone and return wouldn't be the end of the world and Calliope was perfectly capable of taking care of herself.

Keep saying it over and over, Seph. Maybe you'll learn to believe it. Only made worse when, as I exited the room, an email landed.

I'm very concerned about Thalia's bloodwork, Dr.

Sandra Jessup sent. *Can you call me?*

I dialed the number she'd shared and heard her answer after one ring.

"Ms. Pringle," she said, sounding wide awake and perky despite the early morning hour. How was it suddenly 5AM? "I've reviewed the preliminary bloodwork you sent, as well as Thalia's MRI, and I have to say, I'm very worried."

Was the tech who read her scan wrong then? "Is it the tumor?"

"Not at all," Dr. Jessup said. "In fact, from what I can see she's healing perfectly. But there's a heavy dose of something in her blood that the lab hasn't identified yet. Not a sedative or any anti-depressant or anti-psychotic they know of."

Wait, was someone giving her something not on her chart? "Dr. Jessup, could that unknown medication cause hallucinations or a psychotic break?"

"Without knowing what she's been given specifically," she said, "I can't tell you for certain, but I can tell you there are any number of drugs that can cause such issues, especially in someone recovering from brain surgery. But none of them are legal."

You don't say. "Like what?" I wasn't jumping to conclusions, and I knew one person in this place who used to sell drugs and who she sold them to. But why would Nora want to hurt Thalia?

"Methamphetamine," Dr. Jessup said, "that would be at the top of my list. Along with a psychedelic drug like LSD or even one of the more common club choices. Ecstasy—MDMA--comes to mind. All of those can induce psychosis and in Thalia's state, with her low body weight and already weakened state? I'd say that's a distinct possibility." She huffed a breath as I absorbed what she said with a faint euphoria of relief. "I'm so sorry, Ms. Pringle. I'm taking full responsibility for this mess and I'm already in touch with the review board." Okay, she was off the hook with me. "Dr. Yonan has a lot to answer for."

Tell me about it. "Thank you, Dr. Jessup." She had no idea how much better she made me feel. "I'll be in touch." I hung up and briefly considered going back into the room to talk to the girls, to reassure them both. Instead, I decided to wrap this case up first and then deal with Thalia.

The truth remained she may have killed Asher after all. But at least now she had a solid defense. If I could prove someone else was dosing her.

I texted Boone the moment I made my choice and headed down the hallway, but when no response was imminent, I went looking for him instead. Found the two uniforms at the front entry guarding Jose, obviously waiting for someone to come and pick him up.

"Is Detective Boone outside?" I needed my coat if so.

"The techs aren't here yet," the male uniform said.

"We'd be happy to share any information you have with him," the female officer told me, audibly and visibly not happy in the least.

I considered handing the evidence over and

changed my mind. "If you see him, tell him I'm looking for him. It's important." I shoved the camera under Jose's nose. "Is this what you're missing?"

His eyes widened a little and he nodded. "That's it," he said.

"Tell me," I threw at him before the two officers, now concerned, could interrupt, "what exactly have you been giving Thalia to make her crack like that?" He flinched, guilt written all over him while inside I crowed in victory. "Meth, Jose? Molly?" I was ready to scream and hug myself and punch him in the face all at the same time as he glanced sideways at the cops before muttering his answer.

"Ecstasy," he said, the other street slang for MDMA clinching the truth with the clang of prison bars because he was going away for a long, long time. "But it was Asher's idea. And he brought the drugs with him."

Like that made a bit of difference, though it did mean Nora had nothing to do with it, thankfully. "You drugged Asher last night, didn't you?" Jose didn't answer aside from his baleful glare. "You're still lying. I'm done with it. Tell me the truth. You jabbed him with the same drugs you were giving Thalia. Admit it."

Jose's lips puckered before he grunted and bobbed a hard nod. "I didn't kill him," he said. "I just wanted him to know I was serious." His demeanor changed somewhat, the rigidity of his body loosening, his rounded shoulders sagging as he dropped his head, aggressive tone fading to a near-whisper. "I went to see him, and he refused to pay me again, so I jabbed him. He didn't even feel it, thought I squeezed his shoulder. I left and watched as he argued with Dr. Yonan. I went around the back way, caught up with Asher at the door to the greenhouse. He was so out of it." Jose shook his head. "But he threatened me, still refused to pay."

"So, you opened the door and pushed him down the stairs," I said. "Knowing you'd just dosed Thalia and she wouldn't remember a thing."

Jose opened his mouth as if to argue, but I wasn't done.

"You tampered with the camera outside." He didn't comment. "And the footage from earlier. That makes you look guilty, Mr. Delgato." Again his silence dominated. That only made things worse for me, not better, his lack of information infuriating. But no more so than my need to know the answer to my final question. "Why did you dose her again after Asher died?" My frustration had peaked, the utter uselessness of the act making me shake with rage. "Why bother perpetuating the lie she was sick?"

Jose just shook his big head. "I want a lawyer. I'm done talking. I know when I'm being railroaded."

Whatever. I backed off, scowling at both officers. The woman seemed inclined to demands, her gaze locked on the nanny cam in my hand, but instead of giving her space to claim the evidence, I spun and marched away, ending up in the café.

I needed time to breathe and think. Paced a moment, waiting to hear from Boone, but nothing. Weird, right? Fine, if he wasn't going to join me, the least I could do was prove I was right and hand him

Jose on a silver platter.

The little cable for the camera connected easily with the mic port on my phone and it was a simple matter of downloading the app from my store to review the footage. I was sweating and anxious by the time the green circle finished its round and the app opened. I knew exactly what time code to look for, scanned through the recordings rapidly, and found exactly when I was seeking.

Sighed heavily in frustration when the camera's view pointed, not at the door, but at Thalia standing over her plants. Which meant this footage was useless, too. Until Asher flew into the scene, crashing to the steps. I was spared the moment of his death as his wheelchair took out the pot the camera had been hidden in, spinning the lens around and shifting its perspective to aim, with the greatest luck ever, right at the doorway.

Which had me staring in shock and growing horror at the sight of who it was that pushed Asher Wyatt to his death.

I spun and sprinted out of the café, heading for the residences. Checked the room in question, found it empty. As I raced out into the lobby for help, I realized the cops and Jose were already gone. Leaving me without backup.

I was on my own, then. But the question remained as I took the hallway to the offices, where the hell was Boone?

CHAPTER TWENTY-FIVE

You know how sometimes you ask a question and get an answer you really wish you hadn't? That was me as I stormed to the end of the corridor to the reception desk and past it, pushing through the entry to Dr. Yonan's office, the light on luring me to a confrontation.

Just not the one I was expecting. Because when I wondered where Boone was? I hadn't expected to find him in the very place I'd gone looking. Or with Dr. Yonan behind his desk, hands held up.

With the very lovely and deadly Faith Yale pointing a gun at them both.

Then again, since I'd just seen her push Asher down the stairs and watch him die... "Faith," I said, pulling myself up short but far too late to exit as her gun hand whipped around and she pointed the very dangerous looking pistol in my direction. "It's over, Faith. I have proof of what you did." I held up the small camera to Boone. "I've sent it to the authorities." Liar, but did she know that? "There's no way out now, my dear. Please, put the gun down. It's time to tell the truth."

"It is," she said, almost wailed, tears streaming down her face as she repositioned the gun to hover at chest height on Dr. Yonan. He was clearly going to be useless to us, seated as he was, face caught between terror and agony, unable to move without catching a bullet. Faith's whole being might have been weakened by her disease, but her gun hand was rock steady. "It's time, Amir. You never loved me. You're going to leave me and lie about us and say it was all me. I know it!"

"I would never," he spluttered even as I read the deception in his face, the way his gaze flickered to me and back to her again before locking on the muzzle of the gun. "I swear—"

She shook a sheet of paper at him that had rested in her lap, the wheelchair in which she sat doing nothing to make her less threatening. If anything, her condition made her desperate and that meant she had nothing to lose. Not a great position to start negotiating with her from. Like she was in the mood to negotiate. "I found your email to the board," she snarled. "I read it, all of it. How could you?" She crumpled it and threw it at him, but it missed, bouncing off the edge of the desk and rolling to my feet. I bent and unfolded it, reading the carefully crafted blame he placed squarely on her, citing proof he said he had and that she was mentally unstable. I didn't bother finishing the litany written in Ph.D.speak, because it turned my stomach. Instead, I tossed it to the ground myself, fixing Yonan with a scowl.

"You have to know you'd never get away with it," I said. "Not after what I've seen." Yonan sat there mute and without excuses for the moment. Smart man. "Faith," I said, "he's not worth it."

She choked on a bitter laugh. "I know that now," she said. "I came in here to prove to myself he loved me, to erase all of our emails, all of the messages I sent. And what do I find open in a new document?" She slammed her free fist down on the arm of her chair, rattling the frame. There was strength in her yet. "How could you do this to me?"

"I'm sorry," he whispered, though more for getting caught than hurting her, I had no doubt.

"We know you are," Boone said then, soft and caring, pouring on his authentic game with as much compassion as he could muster. It was a lot, too. I was impressed. But if he could fake that, what else could he fake? "We want to help you, Faith."

"Shut up." She flashed the gun at him, lips twisting in bitter fury. "All of you men are alike."

"Aren't they." I dug deep for resentment and found it, Faith looking up at me in surprise. "What, you expect me to argue? I was married to a man who can't even bring himself to comfort his own daughter now that he has a new family to care about." Wow, Seph, say it like you mean it. This was supposed to be an act, not a confessional, but nothing short of truth was going to reach her, I was sure of that, so I let it all out and hoped claiming it a ruse later would save my honor. "Oh, and how about the man who turned out to be a murderer and an international assassin who wanted to kill me as much as be with me?" Sorry, Gaines. "Or the so-called journalist who used me to get to my daughter and Thalia and twist everything he learned to sell his stupid magazine?" I had no idea I'd been holding onto this much anger. "The worst? The guy who up and died on me and made me the prime suspect in his death. Men suck, Faith."

She blinked at me, nodding. "You get it," she said.

"I do." I faced her squarely, ignoring the men. "No one is saving Amir, Faith. No one. He's going down for what he did. I promise you that." She quivered, lower lip trembling. Was she having second thoughts? I had her rattled, now to pounce. "I know what you did, Faith. But why?"

"To protect him," she jabbed the gun at Dr. Yonan again. "Asher was going to tell. I couldn't let that happen. So, when I found him in the hallway by the greenhouse door, I took advantage of the situation. He was babbling, out of it. I figured he self-dosed on something he brought with him. Wouldn't be the first time." Her revulsion had me wondering how broken she was since she had her own means of punishment that involved food, not drugs, but this was no time to quibble. "I didn't set out to kill him, just to talk to him. He was right there, and he wouldn't listen and I just…" she shivered, eyes glazing over, clearly reliving the moment. I almost made a move, was on the cusp of lunging for the gun, when she snapped out of it and looked up at me again. "I didn't think. I just did it."

"Did you mean to kill him?" My only choice was to talk her down.

"No," she whispered. Paused and bit her lip. "Maybe."

"It was an accident," I said, as soothing as possible, nodding and smiling sadly to her while she seemed to cling to my words. "You didn't set out to hurt anyone. Sure, maybe you wanted him to get hurt in the moment, but that's not a crime." Um, well, it was, but semantics and broken girls with weapons. I was doing my best.

"It's his own fault he died," she said then, brightening somewhat, wiping at her face with her free hand. "If he'd been sober, he would be alive. That little push shouldn't have killed him." Wow, and here I thought I was good at talking people out of things. She was a master, at least of her own excuses. She sighed softly and lowered the gun just a little. "This is all your fault." She spun on Dr. Yonan again, only this time without the tears or the heartbreak. Nope, she was all hardcore threatening all the time.

So much for my excellent therapy skills.

"Now what?" I kept my voice soft and conversational, kindly even. My best office voice. "Faith, so far so good. We've decided that." Or at least, she had. Her big eyes returned to fix on me.

"But if you hurt him, that's it. You have to know it. If you kill Dr. Yonan, there's no going back."

She looked back and forth between us, the gun still pointing at the doctor. "I can't let him get away with it."

"He won't, remember?" I brightened my smile, holding my own hand out. "I've got you. Let me take care of him. I promise he's done."

"You'll make him suffer?" She sobbed then, the gun held out toward me. I rushed to her side, freeing it from her hand and instantly passing it off to Boone who was beside me before I could turn to offer it up to him. And then I was hugging Faith and she was clinging to me while Dr. Yonan leaped to his feet and ran for the door, Boone catching him before he could exit.

"It's okay now," I lied to Faith who really needed me to in that moment. "Everything is going to be all right.

Her bitter weeping told me she knew better but wasn't fighting it. Instead, she let me support her and give her a moment of grace before she accepted her fate.

To Boone's credit, he let her cry herself out before he arrested her for murder.

CHAPTER TWENTY-SIX

My coffee machine burbled happily as it poured out a steady stream of aromatic java, bacon and eggs merrily bubbling in the frying pan while the sound of the girls laughing over music upstairs added a final layer to the lovely symphony of happy life that filled my house with joy.

I poured myself a cup and sipped, enough cream and sugar to soften the edge of the dark roast pure bliss that encouraged me to lean into the counter and stare out the window into the backyard and the skiff of snow that had fallen overnight. It wouldn't stay, far too early for the white stuff to linger, but it was nice to see the clean white layer over everything as if the fall had hidden everything that didn't fit under a perfect coating of sparkling light.

My phone buzzed, the text's sender making me smile, and not just because of the long message he sent. I read through Detective Kellan Boone's kindly update with a little thrill inside me that distracted from the news he delivered.

Thought you'd like to know, partner, he sent, the sound of his voice absent but loud and clear in my mind regardless. *Faith Yale is being charged with manslaughter instead of murder, among other things. Turns out she was the one who erased the footage. Yonan gave her far too much access to the back offices during their trysts. But, from what I hear she's pleading guilty. As for Dr. Yonan, he's losing his license, you're welcome.* I grinned at that, a tight and vengeful expression I was glad no one was present to see. Not befitting a therapist, but I was also a protective mother, right? The latter took precedence in this particular case. *The whole facility is under investigation, and the Wyatts are trying to distance themselves, but I have a feeling there'll be repercussions there, too.* They had lost their son, even if he was an evil little jerk, so I didn't wish them all ill. Still, it had been their demon spawn who'd been the source of Thalia's issues, so I struggled to empathize. Again, glad I was alone. *Jose Delgato confessed to everything, including knocking out the back stair camera for Asher. He says he kept drugging Thalia because he was trying to distract us. When Gray caught him at it, he knew it was time to ditch, but needed the camera. If you hadn't caught him, he might have gotten away, so that one's yours.* Nice of him to share credit. *I know you disagree, but Luca Diaz is still on my radar. You told me he's a good kid, and he probably is, but his family warrants my attention for as long as he remains at the facility.* I wasn't going to argue that point. *Nora Teres is off the hook, though. As long as she stays on the straight and narrow and doesn't go back to selling drugs, I'm giving her a pass. You're also welcome.* I smiled again. A man who listened, imagine. *Jose Delgato will serve hard time, though there's no sign of Gray Fender, so I assume he's crawled back into the ooze he wriggled his way out of.* That did raise a frown. The so-called journalist might not have done anything wrong technically, I wasn't all that fond of his tactics and the reminder Thalia's delicate health still warranted protectiveness and shielding her from negativity, I dreaded anything he might decide to publish. But so far, so good. When I'd checked the newest posts for Truth or Bare, while Gray had outed The Recovery Center in a giant, splashy expose that made Dr. Yonan look like the creep he was, nothing had been mentioned about Thalia.

As long as Gray kept his distance, I'd keep mine.

Boone wasn't done. *Thanks for all the help,* he sent. *I meant what I said. I think you're remarkable. I never thought I'd be ready for someone to come into my life, but maybe that's the point. We're never ready.* Maybe he was right. *I'd love to work with you again.* I almost choked on the word, spitting out some of my coffee with my eyes widening. Love? Okay, Seph, stop with the conclusion jumping already. It was just a word. *Either that or take you to dinner. Or both. You decide and I'll be here when you're ready.*

Well, now. I could eat.

I was pondering what to say in response when an email landed, this one from Dr. Sandra Jessup and I immediately dove into it, Boone on the side burner for the moment.

Thalia is in the clear, she sent. *Now that she's no longer being illegally dosed, her bloodwork is perfect and she's in excellent health. All tests came back negative for cancer. The cyst was benign. We'll keep an eye on her for the foreseeable future with scans and further tests, but it's exciting news. I wish Thalia the very best, and I hope she can forgive me for my part in this. I'm meeting with the board this week to discuss Amir Yonan. If I'm no longer able to be Thalia's doctor moving forward, I do hope she recovers fully and never needs my services again regardless.*

I made a note to myself to contact the medical board directly. Dr. Jessup didn't need to throw herself under the bus for something Yonan was responsible for, and I was going to make sure the ruling body knew so.

In the meantime, however, the weight of the truth about Thalia had me shaking. I blinked away some tears as I let out a hitching breath of relief, not realizing I'd been hanging onto that grief and worry still despite having Thalia home with us and knowing the source of her instability. So much for the Vesterville curse. I fired off a thank you to Dr. Jessup and set my phone aside, letting my heart heal as I finished breakfast for my girls.

I was loading the food onto a tray when my phone buzzed one last time. The source of the text had my mood shifting from happy contentment to irritation.

I've been held up, Gaines Vesterville sent. Yeah, no kidding. Thalia's disappointment he'd failed to appear wasn't helping matters, though she seemed content to wait for his pending arrival with optimism. I wasn't so gracious. *Thank you for taking care of her. And keeping me up to date. I know you don't believe it, but she means everything to me. There are times when me keeping my distance is my best way of protecting her.*

Okay, I understood that. He was an international spy and assassin and wasn't exactly an excellent role model. Still, he was all the blood relation she had left.

Gaines would arrive or not in his own time. The most important part? Thalia was healthy and would stay that way if I had anything to do or say about it. And as for Kellan Boone... well, dinner sounded nice, didn't it?

Humming to myself, tray loaded with toast, jam and a pile of eggs and bacon, I headed upstairs, pausing at Callie's bedroom door. It stood open, the pair of them giggling and chattering together with Belladonna firmly ensconced between them, all three looking up at my arrival. And knew, in that instant, no matter what, bringing Thalia home was the best decision I'd ever made.

"Who's hungry?"

Looking for the next Persephone Pringle mystery?
Find book eight, *Till Death Sue Us Part*, available
now!

PERSEPHONE PRINGLE COZY MYSTERIES: EIGHT

PATTI LARSEN

TILL DEATH SUE US PART

ABOUT THE AUTHOR

Everything you need to know about me is in this one statement: I've wanted to be a writer since I was a little girl, and now I'm doing it. How cool is that, being able to follow your dream and make it reality? I've tried everything from university to college, graduating the second with a journalism diploma (I sucked at telling real stories), am an enthusiastic member of an all-girl improv troupe (if you've never tried it, I highly recommend making things up as you go along as often as possible) and I get to teach and perform with an amazing group of women I adore. I've even been in a Celtic girl band (some of our stuff is on YouTube!) and was an independent filmmaker (go check out the Lovely Witches Club). My life has been one creative thing after another—all leading me here, to writing books for a living.

Now with multiple series in happy publication, I live on beautiful and magical Prince Edward Island (I know you've heard of Anne of Green Gables) with my multitude of pets.

I love-love-love hearing from you! You can reach me (and I promise I'll message back) at https://patti@pattilarsen.com. And if you're eager for your next dose of Patti Larsen books (usually about one release a month) come join my mailing list! All the best up and coming, giveaways, contests and, of course, my observations on the world (aren't you just dying to know what I think about everything?) all in one place: https://bit.ly/PattiLarsenEmail.

Last—but not least!—I hope you enjoyed what

you read! Your happiness is my happiness. And I'd love to hear just what you thought. A review where you found this book would mean the world to me—reviews feed writers more than you will ever know. So, loved it (or not so much), your honest review would make my day. Thank you!